MID-CONTINENT PUBLIC LIBRARY
15616 E. 24 HWY
INDEPENDENCE, MO 64050

3 0 0 0 4 0 0 2 0 4 9 5 9 7

14

"You ha⋯⋯⋯⋯ s been."

"Dare I hope," she gasped, clutching her heart, making him laugh. Shaking her head, she smiled. "There's no way this truce is going to last."

"I'll try if you will," he said, his eyes twinkling with mischief, and she had to laugh in return.

"I'll try, I promise."

"I keep waiting for a pitch from you to get me to agree to something. You all but admitted that was the purpose of your bidding for me tonight at the auction."

"Maybe I've shelved that original agenda," she said in a sultry voice. "I'm having fun, Tony. Fun that I don't want to spoil. The night is magical. For a few hours, let's enjoy it."

He raised her hand and brushed a light kiss on her knuckles. His breath was warm.

"I'm glad you feel that way," he said. "I'm not ready to tell you good-night and watch you walk away."

* * *

That Night with the Rich Rancher is part of the Lone Star Legends series from *USA TODAY* bestselling author S⋯⋯ig!

D1538393
⋯E
⋯ARY

Dear Reader,

When love fills the heart, there is no room for hatred. This love story, about reconciliation, attraction and forgiveness, involves billionaire rancher Tony Milan and his rancher neighbor, Lindsay Calhoun. Tony has a cowboy's deep appreciation for a beautiful woman, an appreciation that transcends angry disputes and a long-standing family feud.

Two Texas families with their feud, their legends, their loves and their close family ties have their final story as Tony and Lindsay each find the other irresistible in spite of all their differences. Tony, who is always ready for fun, is dazzled by Lindsay, whose life revolves around her family and her precious horses and dogs.

It's bittersweet for me as a writer to say farewell to the Milans and Calhouns in this final story about their families and their century-old feud. I hope you enjoy sharing this story with them, too.

Sara Orwig

WITHDRAWN
FROM THE RECORDS OF THE
MID-CONTINENT PUBLIC LIBRARY

THAT NIGHT WITH
THE RICH RANCHER

———

SARA ORWIG

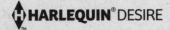

If you purchased this book without a cover you should be aware
that this book is stolen property. It was reported as "unsold and
destroyed" to the publisher, and neither the author nor the
publisher has received any payment for this "stripped book."

Recycling programs
for this product may
not exist in your area.

ISBN-13: 978-0-373-73436-8

That Night with the Rich Rancher

Copyright © 2016 by Sara Orwig

All rights reserved. Except for use in any review, the reproduction or
utilization of this work in whole or in part in any form by any electronic,
mechanical or other means, now known or hereinafter invented, including
xerography, photocopying and recording, or in any information storage
or retrieval system, is forbidden without the written permission of the
publisher, Harlequin Enterprises Limited, 225 Duncan Mill Road,
Don Mills, Ontario M3B 3K9, Canada.

This is a work of fiction. Names, characters, places and incidents are
either the product of the author's imagination or are used fictitiously,
and any resemblance to actual persons, living or dead, business
establishments, events or locales is entirely coincidental.

This edition published by arrangement with Harlequin Books S.A.

For questions and comments about the quality of this book,
please contact us at CustomerService@Harlequin.com.

® and TM are trademarks of Harlequin Enterprises Limited or its
corporate affiliates. Trademarks indicated with ® are registered in the
United States Patent and Trademark Office, the Canadian Intellectual
Property Office and in other countries.

Printed in U.S.A.

Sara Orwig lives in Oklahoma. She has a patient husband who will take her on research trips anywhere, from big cities to old forts. She is an avid collector of Western history books. With a master's degree in English, Sara has written historical romance, mainstream fiction and contemporary romance. Books are beloved treasures that take Sara to magical worlds, and she loves both reading and writing them.

Books by Sara Orwig

Harlequin Desire

Stetsons & CEOs

Texas-Sized Temptation
A Lone Star Love Affair
Wild Western Nights

Lone Star Legacy

Relentless Pursuit
The Reluctant Heiress
Midnight Under the Mistletoe
One Texas Night...
Her Texan to Tame

Lone Star Legends

The Texan's Forbidden Fiancée
A Texan in Her Bed
At the Rancher's Request
Kissed by a Rancher
The Rancher's Secret Son
That Night with the Rich Rancher

Visit the Author Profile page
at Harlequin.com, or
saraorwig.com, for more titles.

With many thanks to Stacy Boyd, Senior Editor

One

Tony Milan felt ridiculous. Standing in the wings of the wide stage of the elegant Dallas country club ballroom, he promised himself that next time, he would be more careful making bets with his oldest brother. Losing at saddle bronc riding in a rodeo last April had put him backstage tonight at this gala charity event, which included a dinner dance as well as an auction. One that would auction *him* off. At least it was all for a good cause, he reminded himself. The funds raised would go to Parkinson's disease research.

As he'd made his way to the stage earlier, he had seen some of the attendees: beautiful women dressed in designer gowns accompanied by men in tailored tuxedos. The highest bidders would win a night with "Texas's most desirable bachelors," according to the brochure that had been mailed to a select group wealthy enough to afford the event. He couldn't imagine any woman bidding much for an evening out with a guy she won in an auction, but after the opening bid, he realized he was wrong. The Texas ranchers who'd gone before him had stirred up high prices.

Looking out at the latest bachelor who now pranced offstage, Tony could not recall ever feeling more out of place. And then he heard his name called.

Taking a deep breath and forcing himself to smile broadly, he stepped forward, striding out of the darkened shadows into the blinding spotlights in front of a glittering audience. Applause was loud as he waved at the audience, most of which he could no longer clearly see because of the spotlights shining in his eyes.

After a spiel about his bachelor status, the master of ceremonies opened up the bidding. Tony was startled by the number of women who jumped into the bidding, but as the amount climbed, first one and then another dropped out until only three women were left.

Shocked yet pleased by the amount he was going to draw, he grinned and walked around the stage as the bidding climbed.

When a woman in a front table bid, he glanced down and saw it was an ex-girlfriend. He hoped she didn't win. As far as he was concerned, he'd said a final goodbye to her when she'd started getting serious. No long-term relationships for Tony Milan. He liked to flirt, play the field, just have a good time with no strings attached. Thankfully, after a flurry of bidding, his ex-girlfriend dropped out and only two women were left.

Tony couldn't see either one of the women, hidden by the blinding lights, but he heard their competitive bids. They were calling outrageous sums of money—all for an evening with him. When one graciously dropped out, the MC brought down the gavel.

"We have a winner," he said, not able to hide his out-right glee at the final amount for the charity. "Would our lucky woman please come up onto the stage?"

Tony couldn't contain his curiosity. He scanned the audience for a glimpse at her, and then a spotlight found her at a table off to the right. His pulse jumped when a stunning blonde stood up. Her hair was piled atop her head with a few spiral curls falling about her face, and she wore a fiery red dress as she threaded her way to the stage. Even from a distance he could see the dress clung to a breathtaking figure. Jeweled straps glittered on her slender shoulders and her full breasts pillowed above the low-cut neckline.

One of the auction's ushers took her hand as she climbed the steps to the stage and Tony's gaze finally swept over her from head to toe, taking in her long, shapely legs revealed by a high slit in the skirt. Instantly Tony began to feel immensely better about the entire auction and the upcoming evening.

As the blonde crossed the stage, his gaze swept over her features. She wasn't a local resident, he thought, be-cause he didn't recognize her. But then as she neared center stage to give the MC her name, he had a niggling feeling that he did indeed know her. He looked at her again. Something about her features seemed familiar. Perhaps… There was a faint resemblance to a local—his neighbor and lifetime enemy, Lindsay Calhoun.

He shrugged away that notion. The woman talking to the MC could not be Lindsay Calhoun. For one brief moment, a memory flashed through his mind of Lindsay dressed in skintight jeans and driving her muddy pickup, her long sandy braid bouncing beneath her floppy old hat. That was followed by another memory—Lindsay wag-ging her finger at him and accusing him of taking her ranch's water—something unethical he would never do to any neighbor, even Lindsay. She was mule stubborn, never took his advice and wouldn't agree with him if he said the sun set in the west.

Most of all, she was serious in every way, all business all the time. With their many confrontations, he had wondered if she'd ever had any fun in her life. So there was no way on earth that the vision who had won an evening with him was Lindsay.

Curiosity ran rampant as the MC took the mystery woman's hand and she turned to the audience, shooting a quick glance at Tony and then smiling at the audience while the MC held her hand high like a boxer at a heavyweight fight.

"Our winner—a beautiful Texan, Miss Lindsay Calhoun!"

Tony was stunned. His gaze raked over her again. Why had she done this? Their families had maintained a perpetual feud since the first generation of Milans and Calhouns had settled in Texas, and he and Lindsay kept that feud alive. Besides, she didn't even date. Nor would she spend a dime for an evening with him. She never even spoke to him unless she was accusing him of something.

He squeezed his eyes shut as if to clear them, and then looked at her again. Actually, he stared, transfixed. Not one inch of her looked like his neighbor.

She turned as another man in a black tux came forward to escort her toward Tony while the MC began to talk about the next bachelor.

"Lindsay?" Tony's voice came out a croak. The woman he faced was breathtaking. He wouldn't have guessed all the makeup in Texas could have made such a transformation.

Her huge blue eyes twinkled and she leaned close, giving him a whiff of an exotic perfume—another shock.

"Close your mouth, Tony," she whispered so only he could hear. "And stop staring."

The tuxedo-clad man stepped forward. "Lindsay, it seems you've already met your bachelor, Tony Milan. Tony, this is Lindsay Calhoun."

"We know each other." Tony hoped he said it out loud. His brain felt all jumbled and he couldn't force his gaze from Lindsay. He still couldn't believe what he was seeing. He had known her all his life. Not once had she even caused him to take a second glance. Nor had he ever seen her as anything except a colossal pest. Saying she wasn't his type was an understatement.

But was there another side to her? Why was Lindsay here? Why had she bid a small fortune to get the evening with him? No doubt she wanted something from him— and wanted it badly.

Would she go to this length to get water? He ruled that out instantly, remembering her fury and harsh words when she had accused him of buying bigger pumps for his wells to take more groundwater from the aquifer they shared. He had told her what she should do—dig her wells deeper. She had charged right back, saying she wouldn't have to go to the added expense if he wasn't depleting her water with bigger pumps. And there it went. Once again her usual stubborn self refused to take his advice or believe him.

Then she had started calling him devious, a snake and much worse. She pushed him to the edge and he knew he had to just walk away, which he did while she hurled more names at him.

That was the Lindsay Calhoun he knew. This Lindsay tonight had to be up to something, too. Surprisingly, though, he couldn't bring himself to care much. Thoughts of ranching and feuding fled from his mind. He was too busy enjoying looking at one of the most beautiful women he had ever seen.

How could she possibly look so good? They were being given the details of their evening, beginning with a limousine waiting at the country club entrance to take them to the airport where a private jet would fly them to Houston for dinner. He barely registered a word said to him; he couldn't focus on anything but the sight of her.

"Excuse me a moment. I'll be right back," their host said, leaving them alone momentarily.

"You've got to give me a moment to come out of my shock," Tony said with a shake of his head.

"You take all the time you want. I've been waiting for this," she drawled. "If necessary, I would have paid a lot more to get this night with you."

"If you'd come over to the ranch dressed the way you are now and just knocked on the door, you could have had my full attention for an evening without paying a nickel, but this is for a good cause."

"It's for two good causes," she said in a sultry voice, and his heartbeat quickened. He still couldn't quite believe what was happening. Before tonight, he would have bet the ranch he could never be dazzled or even take a second look, let alone willingly go out with his stubborn neighbor.

"Lindsay, I've never fainted in my life, but I might in the next thirty seconds, except I don't want to stop looking at you for anything."

"When you saw I had won, I was afraid you'd turn down this evening."

"I wouldn't turn down tonight if I had to pay twice

what you did," he said without thinking, and her smile widened, a dazzling smile he had never seen in his life.

"If you two will follow me, I can show you to the front entrance," their host said, returning to join them. "First, Miss Calhoun, you need to step to the desk to make arrangements about payment."

"Certainly," she answered. "See you in a few minutes, Tony," she added in a soft, breathless voice.

Where had that sexy tone come from? He recalled times when he had heard her shout instructions to hands on her ranch. She had a voice that could be heard a long stretch away and an authoritative note that got what she wanted done. As he watched her, she turned to look at him. She smiled at him, another dazzling, knee-weakening smile, and he couldn't breathe again.

Holy saints, where had Lindsay gotten that enticing smile? It muddled his thoughts, sent his temperature soaring and made him want to please her enough to get another big smile.

He had seen her stomping around horses, yelling instructions and swearing like one of the men, the sandy braid flopping with her steps. He had faced her when she had yelled furious accusations at him about dumping fertilizer. How could that be the breathtaking woman walking away from him? His gaze ran down her bare back to her tiny waist, down over her flared hips that shifted slightly in a provocative walk.

With the tight dress clinging to her every curve, he caught a flash of long legs when she turned and the slit in her skirt parted. That's when he noticed the stiletto heels. He would have sworn she had never worn heels in her life, yet she moved as gracefully as a dancer. He wiped his heated brow. This was rapidly turning into the most impossible night of his life.

Befuddled, totally dazzled by her, he tried to remind himself she was Lindsay, and he should pull his wits together. That might not be so easy. He would never again view her in the same manner.

Why hadn't he ever really looked at her before? He knew full well the answer to his question. He had been blinded by their fights over every little thing, from her tree falling on his truck to his fence on her property line. Not to mention her usual raggedy appearance when she worked.

If she had gone to such lengths tonight to wring something she wanted out of him, he had better get a grip, because it was going to be all but impossible to say no to the fantastic woman in red standing only yards away and writing a check for thousands of dollars for an evening with him. Not even a night— just a dinner date and maybe some dancing.

But Lindsay Calhoun wasn't interested in dinner dates and ballroom dancing, boot scooting or even barn dances. He eyed her skeptically. To what lengths was she prepared to go tonight to get what she wanted?

He gave up trying to figure her out.

Still, he couldn't take his eyes off her. The skintight red dress left little to the imagination. Why had she hidden her gorgeous figure all these years? Why had she always pulled her hair back in a braid or ponytail? He looked at the beautiful silky blond hair arranged on her head, some strands falling loosely in back. He had never seen her hair falling freely around her face—would he before this night was over?

She looked seductive, like pure temptation, and he knew he should be on his guard, but there was no way he could be defensive with the woman standing only yards away. He wanted her in his arms. He wanted to kiss her.

And, if he was truthful with himself, he wanted to make love to her.

When she finished writing and handing over her check, their host led them to a garden, where they had pictures taken together. As he slipped his arm around her tiny waist while they posed for the camera, the physical contact sizzled. He was so heated he thought he would go up in flames.

He made a mental note to get a picture. His brother-in-law and sister were in the audience, so they had seen her tonight. So was his oldest brother, Wyatt. He was certain Jake Calhoun had seen his sister look this way before, but Wyatt was probably as shocked as he had been.

Talking constantly, their host escorted Lindsay and Tony through the wide front doors of the country club, where a long white limousine waited.

As soon as the door closed on the limo, they were alone, except for the driver on the other side of a partition.

"Maybe you've been using the wrong approach," Tony remarked.

She smiled another full smile that revealed even, white teeth that made him inclined to agree with whatever she said.

"That's what I decided. So we'll see how it helps letting my hair down, getting out of my jeans and into a dress, smiling and being friendly. So far, it seems to be working rather well, don't you think?"

"Absolutely. I don't know why you waited this long. I keep reminding myself not to give you the deed to my ranch tonight."

She laughed with a dazzling, irresistible smile on her lips. "The other way is a more direct approach. You know where you stand."

"And this is a sugarcoated enticement to get what you want?"

"Oh, my, yes. I'm just getting started. When I walked up on stage, I'm sure you wanted to refuse keeping your part of the bargain."

"You're wrong. Not the way you look tonight," he said in a husky voice. "With you in that red dress, there's nothing that would cause me to turn down an evening with you."

When had he reacted like this to a woman? He escorted beautiful women, was friends with them, had them continually around in his life and yet never had he been dazzled senseless as he was tonight. He wouldn't ever have guessed Lindsay could generate such attraction and make him overlook all their battles.

It had to be the shock of who she was that was setting him ablaze. He'd better get a grip on reality and see her as the person he knew her to be. But that wasn't going to happen tonight. His thought processes worked clearly enough to know that.

She smiled sweetly. "Penny for your thoughts."

"I'm wondering why I haven't ever heard from anyone about how gorgeous you can be."

"I suppose because I rarely go out on dates and never with anyone in these parts."

"Why not?"

She shrugged. "I've just never met anyone around here I wanted to go out with very much. And there's nowhere close by here to go dressed up."

"There's Dallas."

With a twinkle in her blue eyes, she answered, "In Dallas, our paths probably wouldn't cross."

"I've known you all my life and I know your family

well. Tonight I feel as if I'm spending the evening with a complete stranger I've just met."

She looked amused. "In some ways, Tony, we are strangers. There's a lot you don't know about me," she said in the breathless, sultry voice that made the temperature in the limo climb again.

"I should have asked you out long ago," he said.

"You know how likely that was to have happened, and what my response would have been."

He nodded. "Our past is better left alone and forgotten tonight."

"We fully agree on that one," she answered as the limo slowed. "Tonight is filled with illusions."

"The way you look is no illusion. You're gorgeous," he said, and was rewarded with another coaxing smile.

The limo turned into the airport and in minutes they slowed to a stop. While the chauffeur held the door, Tony took her arm to escort her to the waiting private jet. The moment he touched her, awareness burned in a fiery current. Her arm was warm, her skin silky smooth. He caught another whiff of her exotic perfume, and he couldn't wait to get her to their destination so he could ask her to dance and have an excuse to hold her in his arms.

In the plane he was aware of how close she sat. It was difficult to keep from staring because her red dress had fallen open, revealing those beautiful, long shapely legs. He took a deep breath.

"I need to keep pinching myself to make sure this is actually happening," he said. "And I keep reminding myself you're the same neighbor I see across the fence with your horses."

"I love my horses. You should come visit and really look at them sometime. I have some fine horses."

"I've seen them across the fence. Everyone in the county knows you have some of the finest horses."

"They're working horses or horses for my riding. I like to ride."

"We have that in common, Lindsay."

"I've never seen you riding just for pleasure."

"If it's for pleasure, I don't ride in the direction of your ranch." He smiled sheepishly. "I figure we're both better off that way."

"We're in agreement there, too," she remarked in a tone that was light and held no rancor.

"Have you attended one of these charity bachelor auctions before?"

"Sure, because it's a good cause." She held up a hand but stopped before it touched his arm. "I don't need to ask, I know you haven't. What prompted you to agree to participate in the auction tonight? You seem to be more the type to just donate the money."

"I lost a bet with Wyatt over bronc riding in an Abilene rodeo."

She laughed. "So because of your brother you're trapped into a night with me now."

"I was filled with thoughts of revenge until you stood up to walk to the stage. Since then, this night has taken the best possible turn."

She smiled. "I must admit I'm pleasantly surprised by your reaction. I never, ever thought I'd hear you say that. But you know, underneath this red dress, I'm still me."

He inhaled deeply, his temperature spiking at her mention of what was beneath the red dress, even though she had intended a different meaning.

He cleared his throat. "I have a feeling I better not say anything about what's underneath your red dress."

She looked as if she held back a laugh. "I knew there

had to be another side to you besides the one I always see. I've wondered how the evening would go and so far, so good. I think, Tony, we've set a record already for the length of time we've been civil to each other."

"I intend to be more than 'civil to each other.' We're just getting started," he said. "Frankly, Lindsay, it's damn difficult to remember that you're the same woman whose ranch adjoins mine. I feel as if I'm with a beautiful woman I've just met," he said softly, taking her hand in his and rubbing her knuckles lightly with his thumb. His brows arched and he turned her hand over to open her palm, looking up at her.

"You have soft hands. I know how you work with the cowboys. You should have hands like mine—with scars, calluses and crooked bones from breaks. How did you get these?" he asked, running his thumb lightly over her palm.

"I wear gloves most of the time," she said. "And I haven't been out working quite as much for the past two weeks because I was shopping for a dress and getting ready for tonight."

Her voice had changed, becoming throaty, losing the humor, and he wondered if she had a reaction to his touch. That idea made the temperature in the limo climb again. He gazed into her big blue eyes. "I hope tonight will be far better than you dreamed possible and worth all the effort you put into it," he said softly, and raised her hand to brush her palm with his lips.

His thumb brushed across her wrist and he felt her racing pulse, making his own pulse jump again in response. As he looked into Lindsay's eyes, he wanted to pull her close and kiss her. He couldn't help the thought that came to mind. How much was this night going to complicate his life?

He couldn't answer his question, but he was glad for the auction and thankful she hoped to win him over with sweet talk. It was a dazzling prospect.

He tried to pour on the charm and avoid any topics about the ranch, their relationship or their families. The feud between their families had been far stronger when they had been children and their grandparents had influenced the families. As a small child, Tony was taught to avoid speaking to any Calhoun, and she'd been taught the same about the Milans. In fact, they hadn't spoken to each other until they became neighboring ranchers and had their first dispute over her tree falling on his fence and hitting his truck.

The plane ride seemed to take mere minutes. Before he knew it, they touched down in Houston and were ushered to another waiting limo. A short while later, they pulled into a circular drive lined by manicured shrubs strung with tiny white lights and stopped in front of a sprawling stone building he recognized as an exclusive club.

When they stepped out of the limo, Tony took her arm to walk through the canopied entrance. Inside, when he told the maître d' they were from the Dallas auction, they were welcomed and led to a linen-covered table by a window overlooking the wide patio that held hundreds more twinkling lights and a splashing water fountain.

A piano player sang as he played a familiar old ballad and several couples danced on a small dance floor.

In minutes they were presented a bottle of Dom Pérignon champagne. As soon as they were alone with drinks poured, Tony raised his glass in a toast. "Here's to the most beautiful woman in Texas."

She smiled. "A very nice exaggeration, Tony," she said, touching his glass lightly with hers and taking a sip. "Actually, you look rather handsome yourself."

He smiled and wondered if she felt any real attraction. "Lindsay, I can't imagine why you've been hiding that beauty all these years."

She laughed. "Not so many years, Tony. And thank you. I'm far from the most beautiful woman in Texas, but it's nice to hear."

"You could have had most of the single guys in the county asking you out if you'd wanted," he said.

"Actually, that's not my aim in life," she remarked. "And I do get asked out."

"To talk about someone's horses. If they could see you tonight, though, horses wouldn't come up in the conversation." He waited a second and then asked the question that flitted into his mind. "Speaking of which, Lindsay, will you go to dinner with me next Friday night?"

She grinned at him. "Aren't you jumping the gun? You don't know if we can make it through tonight and get along the entire time."

He leaned across the table to take her hand again. "I promise you, we're going to get along tonight," he said, his tone lowering as it did when he was aroused. "A lot of people saw you at the auction tonight. I think you'll be inundated with invitations from guys when you get home. I want you to myself," he added softly, and something flickered in the depths of her eyes as her smile vanished and she gazed at him solemnly. Electricity flashed between them, and he wanted to be alone with her and kiss her more than ever.

As their waiter appeared, Tony released her hand and leaned back in his chair, listening to a menu recited by the waiter. When they were alone again, Tony raised his flute of champagne. "Here's to a fabulous evening that we'll both remember and want to repeat."

With a seductive smile, she touched his glass with hers

lightly, causing a faint clink, and sipped again, watching him the whole time with a look that made him want to forget dinner and find somewhere to be alone with her.

"I'm beginning to see that you have a sensual side you've kept well hidden."

"Well, yes, Tony. I've kept it hidden from *you*," she said with good humor, and he laughed.

"I suppose I brought that on," he said, wondering whom she had allowed to see this aspect of herself. He sat back to study her. "As well as I know your family, I really don't know much about you. You went to Texas Tech, didn't you? And you were an agriculture major?"

"Yes, with a minor in business. I knew I'd come home to run a ranch."

"Good background. Do you ever feel overwhelmed with the ranch?"

"Sometimes the problems seem a little overwhelming, but I love the ranch too much to feel at odds with it. It's my life."

"I agree, but it's different for you. Don't you want a family someday?"

"Owning the ranch doesn't mean I can't have a family," she retorted.

"I suppose." He nodded as he considered her remark. "Everyone in the county knows you work as hard as the guys who work for you. It's difficult to look at you now and remember how tough and resilient you are."

"Did you know my big brother came out to the ranch, sat me down and lectured me to try to get me to be nicer to you?"

"The hell you say. Is that why you're here tonight?" he asked. Still, he couldn't believe that the gorgeous creature flirting with him now was only here to make nice.

She leaned over the table, reaching out to take his

hand in hers, and his heart jumped again. Every touch, her flirting, the looks she was giving him, all stirred responses that shocked him. No other woman had ever had the same instant effect on him from the slightest contact.

"No," she replied, her voice lowering. "Before the night is over, you'll know this was all my idea and not one of my brothers had anything to do with my plans for tonight."

Her plans? His mind began to race with the possibilities and they were all X-rated. His blood pulsed hot through his veins. "I'm beginning to wish we were alone right now."

With a satisfied expression, she sat back. "Mike and Josh weren't at the auction and I haven't talked to them lately. They have no idea what I'm doing tonight. Jake was in the audience, with Madison, but across the room from me. Otherwise, I'm sure he would have tried to stop my bidding because he would have suspected my motives. But he more than any of my brothers should know you can take care of yourself."

Tony nodded. "I'll bet it was Jake who tried to talk you into being nicer. Mike has had his own problems with losing his first wife, caring for four-year-old Scotty and getting married to Savannah. And Josh is too busy making money with his hotels."

"You're right about all three." She glanced down to their joined hands. "Although I don't think this was exactly what Jake had in mind when he told me to be civil to you."

Tony couldn't help but smile. "I'm sure it wasn't." He turned his hand so that his was holding hers and rubbed his thumb across her smooth skin. "You know, I've heard little Scotty adores his aunt Lindsay. I'm beginning to see how that's possible."

"I don't think Scotty sees me the way you do."

He laughed. "No, I'm sure he doesn't. But you have a whole different side to you that I'm seeing tonight." And he was still having quite a time wrapping his mind around this Lindsay. If this auction night had happened when she first moved to her ranch, would they have avoided their big clashes? Or would that same stubborn Lindsay still have been lurking beneath this beauty?

"I've gotten the same lecture from my brother Wyatt about cooling our fights," he told her. "As county sheriff, he just wants peace and quiet in his life and he doesn't want to have to continually deal with our battles—which will be less in the future, I promise you."

"I hope we can end the clashes altogether."

"If you're like this, you'll have my complete cooperation. You know, I have to tell you. Over the years, some things you've wanted or accused me of destroying, I had nothing to do with. Hopefully, after this, you'll listen to my side a little more. But enough about our past. It doesn't exist tonight, Lindsay."

"That suits me fine," she said softly as she licked her lower lip.

"That does it." He pushed back his chair and went around to her. "If you do one more sexy thing, I may go up in spontaneous combustion." He held out his hand to her. "Let's dance. I don't want the table between us anymore." He also needed to move around and cool down.

Her blue eyes sparkled. "Ah, so I have your attention."

"You've had my full attention since that spotlight revealed you."

He led her to the dance floor, where he turned to take her into his arms. He was intensely aware of her enticing perfume, of her soft hand in his, of her other hand skimming the back of his neck. She was soft, lithe and a good dancer, one more surprise for the evening.

"You have really hidden yourself away from a lot of fun and a lot of attention."

"I have a life. Around the ranch and in Verity, I don't think I've missed a thing. You don't know what I do when I go to Dallas, Houston or New York."

"No, I don't, but I'm curious now."

"I have a lovely time. I have friends in other places besides Verity and the ranch, you know."

"I'll bet you do," he said, smiling at her.

He had seen Lindsay in one of the bars in Verity, playing poker and downing whiskey like one of the men. Now he had a hard time reconciling that image with the woman in his arms. He stared at her, amazed it was her and wondering how long this facade would last.

Even when she returned to her normal self—and she eventually would—he knew he'd never look at her in the same way again. Discovering there was an enticing side to her changed his entire view of the woman who took life too seriously.

For once, she wasn't so serious and earnest. He knew that was her nature, though, and he warned himself not to have high expectations of partying or lovemaking. She was not the type of woman he wanted to get entangled with, but for tonight he was going to break one of his basic rules of life.

Tonight he was going to stop thinking about the past and their problems. Tonight he was simply going to enjoy being with a stunning woman whose intention was to please him. And he wanted to return the favor.

When the dance ended, he took her hand. "I think our salads have been served. Shall we go back?"

As they ate, he listened attentively while she talked about growing up a Calhoun. She avoided mentioning the family feud or any touchy subject. Instead, she related

childhood memories, college incidents and ranch suc-
cess stories. The whole time she spoke, he couldn't stop
picturing her blond hair long and soft over her shoulders.
He wondered if she would let him take it down later. He
wanted to run his fingers through the long strands, hold
her close and kiss her. He wanted seduction.

Again, he wondered about her plans for the night. She
had surprised him constantly since the bidding began
back at the auction. In a way she was being her most
devious self, but he hoped she never stopped. So far, he
had loved every minute of this night since the spotlight
first picked her out of the crowd.

Over their dinners, which were a thick, juicy steak
cooked to perfection for him and a lobster for her, she
asked about his life, and he shared some stories.

Finally, their desserts were brought out, fancy, beauti-
fully crafted dishes that they both ignored because they
were more interested in each other.

"Would you like to dance again?" he asked when she
sat back.

"Of course."

The piano player had been joined by four more musi-
cians, and the group played a ballad that allowed him to
hold Lindsay close in his arms.

"Remember," he whispered in her ear, "for tonight,
we'll forget our battles."

"I already have," she said, squeezing his hand lightly
and making his breath catch.

The band changed to a fast number and he released
Lindsay reluctantly. Instead of returning to her seat, she
began to dance in front of him, and he followed suit. As
he watched her, he could feel his body heat rising. She was
like a flame, her hips gyrating sensuously, her blue eyes
languid and heated as if thoughts of making love were

inspiring her every movement. She was sexy—another shocking discovery. She had to know the effect she was having on him. While her eyes glittered, a faint, satisfied smile hovered on her face. He wanted to yank her into his arms, lean over her until she held him tightly and plunder her soft mouth.

He danced near the wide glass doors overlooking the veranda. He opened the doors and whirled her through them onto the patio, where warm night air enveloped them.

"We can dance out here?"

"The night has cooled enough and we have this to ourselves," he said, moving to the music that was only slightly muted. He danced out of the light spilling through the glass doors, into the shadows and stopped, looking down at her as she tilted her face up.

She was taller than most women he had gone out with, but still shorter than he was. His eyes adjusted to the August night and he could see her looking up at him as he tightened his arm around her, feeling her softness press against him.

"Ever since you walked across the stage at the country club, I've been wanting to do this." Slowly, inch by inch, he leaned in closer, taking his time to steal the kiss he craved.

He wondered if it would be worth the wait.

Two

As Lindsay gazed into Tony's eyes, her heart thudded—and not just from desire. Wanting his kiss disturbed her because it was not part of her plans for enticing him. Still, there was no denying it. Some crazy chemistry burned between them. Actually being attracted to Tony Milan had not even occurred to her as a remote possibility when she'd initially come up with her plan to get him to be friendly and to influence him to stop overpumping his groundwater, which was taking water from her wells. Somewhere in the back of her mind, a question formed in the sultry haze. Could he have been truthful when he said he wasn't using bigger water pumps?

From the first encounter they were at odds. The initial confrontation was over the boundary between their neighboring ranches. Each had come armed with over a century's worth of documents to prove their property lines. Tony had been the condescending Mr. Know-It-

All, telling her she was wrong and how to run her ranch. He'd changed little since that first meeting. He was still a classic alpha male who had to control everything and when it came to ranching, that attitude was annoying. Tonight, though, was a whole different matter.

She was in control.

Or so she planned.

Right now she had to admit she was nearly speechless, because she had never planned or considered an attraction to Tony. She thought she could have a fun, pleasant evening and get on better footing with him. He had lots of friends, so she figured he had to have a nice side and that's what she hoped to get to know tonight with her bachelor-auction ploy.

She had hoped to entice him, make him see her as a desirable woman, have fun and maybe even share some kisses with him so their battles would not be so bitter and he would stop doing annoying things. Instead, she was breathless around him. An attraction between them that she had not expected had flared to life.

How could he be so attractive to her? She knew already that it was because of his charm, his seductive ways, his same alpha male that annoyed her with his know-it-all, take-charge attitude, but now it thrilled her. It was aimed at her, like a missile locked on its target, and, incredibly, she found it appealing...and sexy. She was definitely seeing him in a whole new way tonight.

Still, she couldn't help feeling her carefully laid-out plan was going off the rails a bit. Now wasn't the time to analyze her feelings, though. Not while she was in his arms. She knew this could never continue past tonight. Feelings for Tony Milan could complicate her life big-time. But for one night only, she would go where her heart and body led her. She could only tilt her head back and go with them. And right now they were taking her closer and closer to Tony. She wanted his kiss.

Her heartbeat raced as her gaze lowered to Tony's mouth, and she closed her eyes when his lips finally touched hers.

All thoughts fled and her heart slammed against her ribs as Tony's warm mouth moved on hers. His lips brushed hers lightly, a tantalizing touch that heightened her need for his kiss. Every inch of her tingled as desire electrified her nerves, hot and intense.

Another warm brush of his lips and she tightened her arm around his waist, sliding her hand behind his neck to wind her fingers in his thick, short hair. Every contact was unique, special, something she'd never expected and would never forget.

His mouth settled on hers, parting her lips as his tongue thrust deep and stroked hers, slowly. It was a kiss to make her moan and cling to him, to make her want him more than was sensible and beyond what she had set as limits for tonight's "date." His kiss set her ablaze with desire, making her quiver for his touch and dare to touch him in kind. How could Tony's kisses do this to her? How could he cause responses that no other man ever had?

Her knees felt weak while desire was too strong. Her heart pounded and she moaned softly against his lips. She felt as if she could kiss him for hours and still want so much more from him. As her hand slipped down over his arm, she felt the hard bulge of solid muscle even through the sleeves of his tux and shirt. The feel of that strength, that powerful maleness, rocked her. She felt as if she was hanging on to her senses by a thread.

What she was doing? Somewhere in her mind the question formed, but her thoughts were too scrambled and hungry with need to articulate an answer.

Nearby voices dimly reached her ears, barely register-

ing in her thought processes. Tony released her slightly
and for a few seconds they stared at each other. He looked
as dazed as she felt, his half-lidded eyes smoky and dark,
his lips wet and smeared with her lip gloss.

His voice was thick and deep when he finally spoke.
"Damn, Lindsay, there's another side to you I never knew.
You're a stranger that I've never met before tonight."

"I think I can say the same thing about you," she whispered. "All I hoped was to get you to talk to me."

He dragged his eyes away from hers and cast a glance
to the side of the veranda. He frowned slightly as voices
grew louder.

"We're not alone out here anymore," he whispered,
still studying her solemnly as if she were the first woman
he had ever kissed. But she knew better than that.

"Logic says we should go inside," she replied without moving. For seconds they continued to stare at each
other until Tony took her arm and led her silently back
inside. The small band was playing another fast number and they moved to the dance floor, stepping out in
time to the throbbing beat. Still stunned by his kiss, she
watched him dance, his black tux jacket swinging open
as he moved with a masculine grace that was sensual,
sexy, his hips gyrating and making her think of being
in bed with him.

She felt her cheeks flame and looked up to meet his
gaze. It was as if he read her mind. Desire was blatant
in his eyes.

The band slipped into a slow ballad and Tony took her
hand, drawing her into his arms to dance close. Their
bodies were pressed together, his hardness against her
curves, and she didn't know how long she'd be able to
stay in his arms like this before she would combust. He
pulled back ever so slightly to look down at her, and she

was caught in his solemn gaze. For the first time, she real-ized his eyes were blue, with green flecks in their depths. He had thick dark brown eyelashes, straight brown hair that was neatly cut and short.

Tony Milan was *handsome*.

Down deep she had always thought that, in spite of how annoyed she had usually been with him. But up close like this now, she could no longer view him in any such detached manner. Not after that kiss. Tony Milan wasn't dime a dozen "handsome." No. He was drop-dead gorgeous.

And she wanted him to kiss her again.

The realization surprised her on top of the other jolt-ing shocks of this night. Was she going to regret her deci-sion to see if she could win him over with enticement and sweetness? It wasn't sweetness Tony was bringing out in her tonight. It was desire. She wanted to be alone with him and she wanted him to kiss her again. She wanted to kiss and hold him, to run her hands over him. There was no way she was going to bed with him—she'd es-tablished that boundary from the start—but she wanted more than she'd originally planned.

The night had lost its sense of reality and become a moment out of time. Everything had changed. Desire was hot, constant. Tony was sexy, virile, charming, ap-pealing, and tonight he was the most desirable man she had ever known.

She had never expected or planned on a night like this one. Since she had decided to own a ranch, she had never wanted to date other ranchers or cowboys. She knew them too well and she didn't want them telling her how to conduct her business on the Rocking L Ranch. She loved her ranch—it was her whole life. No one had the right to come along and tell her how to run it. How many times had Tony done exactly that?

Tonight was different, though. Tony was different. How much would tonight change their relationship as neighboring ranchers? Or would they go back home with the same attitudes they had always had?

She knew she wouldn't and she didn't think he would, either.

And then she couldn't think anymore. Tony moved her hand against his chest and covered it with his own, pulling her even closer, as if wrapping their joined hands in the heat from their bodies. She inhaled the scent of his woodsy aftershave, a musky scent that was all male. She gave herself over to him and let him lead her with his sure steps. They were totally in sync as they moved, their long legs pressed against each other's. The contact was electrifying. She wanted to keep dancing with him for hours, almost as much as she wanted to be alone with him, in his arms and kissing him. Was that where the evening would lead, or would he follow the auction itinerary and go back to the Dallas country club, kiss her goodnight and each of them drive away? To her surprise, that wasn't the way she wanted to end the evening.

For the next hour they danced and she realized Tony was fun to be with when he wanted to be. He had her laughing over things he had done with her brothers over the years. She knew he was friends with them even though they were older. She was the only Calhoun who actively fought with him, but she had always blamed Tony for being such a know-it-all and so uncooperative as a neighbor. For tonight, though, she saw none of that. Far from it. He looked as if he was having a wonderful time and he helped her to have a wonderful time.

There was one rational part of her that cried out a

warning: she needed to remember why she bid on him. She couldn't let her plan backfire on her. When this night was over, she'd still need what she came here for—and that wasn't a relationship with Tony Milan. A relationship was the one thing she needed to avoid at all costs, because it would vastly complicate her life. She was here only to win his friendship so he would discuss their problems with her. If possible, even talk about their water situation.

From her earliest memories she had been taught by her grandparents not to trust Milans. Now her brother had married one and he was blissfully happy. She had to admit that she liked and trusted her sister-in-law Madison. And a distant Calhoun cousin—Destiny—had married a Milan—Wyatt, who was sheriff of Verity. Wyatt had been a shock because he proved untrue everything Lindsay had been taught by her grandparents and mother about Milans. In all her dealings with Wyatt, she had found him to be honest, friendly, fair and definitely trustworthy.

She gazed at Tony's handsome features and wondered if he could be trusted, as well. As they danced, he constantly touched her, looked intently at her. He paid her compliments, got her whatever refreshment she wanted. All his attention, his casual touches, increased her awareness of him, as well as her desire for him. She fought the temptation to tell him that she wanted to go someplace where they could be alone. She had a hotel room in Dallas for the night provided by the auction board. She could invite him back for a drink.

As much as she told herself she wanted to kiss him again, she knew where the kissing might lead. And she couldn't make love with Tony. Difficult as it was to curb her desire, she had no other choice.

Finally, as the band took a break, Tony turned to her.

"It's time for us to meet our chauffeur so we can take the plane back to Dallas. It's all arranged to get us back by midnight, so we should go now."

"Let me pick up my purse," she said.

On their flight home, Tony embodied the perfect gentleman, continuing to surprise her. She'd known he had to have a good side to him, but she'd never expected to be charmed by him or even find him such enjoyable company. Certainly not once had she thought she would be attracted to him or see him as a sexy, exciting man whose kiss set her heart pounding.

As they flew back to Dallas, Tony reached for her hand, holding it in his. "The evening will still be young when we get home. We can go dancing or just go have a drink and talk. Better yet, I have a condo in Dallas. Come back with me. I'll take you to your hotel whenever you want. We can have the place to ourselves."

Eagerness to draw out the evening made it easy to answer. "Let's go to your place," she said. "I don't want tonight to end yet. It's been fun, Tony. I know things will go back somewhat to the way they were because that's reality, but this has been a special night."

"You have no idea how special it has been. Things may go back to sort of like they were, but they won't ever again be the same as before. You'll no longer have an antagonistic neighbor. I promise."

"Dare I hope," she gasped, clutching her heart, making him laugh. Shaking her head, she smiled. "There's no way this truce is going to last."

"I'll try if you will," he said, his eyes twinkling with mischief, and she had to laugh in return.

"I promise I'll try, too," she said, looking into his eyes and again feeling an electrifying current spark between them.

"I keep waiting for a pitch from you to get me to agree to something. You all but admitted that's the purpose of your bidding for me tonight."

"Maybe I've delayed that original agenda," she said in a sultry voice. "I'm having fun, Tony. Fun that I don't want to spoil. The night is magical, a trip into a world that doesn't really exist. But for a few hours, we can pretend it does and enjoy it."

He raised her hand and brushed a light kiss on her knuckles, his breath warm on her hand.

"I'm glad," he said. "I'm not ready to tell you goodnight and watch you walk away." He placed his hands on the arms of her seat, facing her and leaning close, his voice dropping to a whisper as he said, "I want to hold you and kiss you again."

Her heart thudded and for the first time she realized she might be in trouble. Was Tony the one who would get what he wanted out of tonight instead of her? She'd planned to wring concessions from him, but now it seemed he was once again in control and she was under his spell. Not once had it crossed her mind that she could be so beguiled by him.

And she was powerless to stop it.

His gaze lowered to her mouth and suddenly she couldn't get her breath. She tingled, feeling as if she strained to lean closer to him while she actually didn't move at all. He moved closer, until his mouth settled on hers. He kissed her, another kiss that set her heart racing and made her want to move into his lap, wrap her arms around him and kiss for the rest of the flight.

Instead, in seconds—or was it minutes?—she shifted away. "This plane isn't the place," she whispered reluctantly. She had to keep her wits about her. Had to mind her goal of working out her water problem, at least partially. Still, her breath came quick and shallow, matching his own.

Looking at her mouth, he didn't move for a moment and her heart continued to drum a frantic rhythm. He leaned closer to whisper in her ear, "I want to kiss you for hours." His words caused a tremor to rock her. Another shock added to the continual shocks of the night. She had no choice but to admit the truth—she wanted him to kiss her for hours.

As his gaze met hers, he scooted back into his seat and buckled his seat belt again.

When her breathing returned to normal, she tried for conversation.

"Why do you have a condo in Dallas? I thought you were as much into ranching as my brother Mike, that both of you had devoted your lives solely to ranching."

"I'm on two boards that meet in Dallas—for my brothers. Wyatt has recently acquired a bank and I'm on that board. Nick recently became owner of a trucking company with two close friends and I'm on that board, too. In Dallas, I have a small condo and I like having a place of my own I can go relax when I'm in the city. It's convenient even though I don't spend a lot of time there. I don't have a regular staff in Dallas unless I plan to stay a long time, which rarely happens. Then I hire from a local agency to cook and clean."

"That makes sense."

"I spend most of my time on my ranch. When we're back in our regular routines, I'd like for you to come over to the MH Ranch sometime. I have a new horse and I'm boarding a new quarter horse that Josh bought. You're welcome to come see them, ride them and tell me what you think."

"Sure," she said. "I suspect you better let all the guys

who work for you know that you invited me or they'll tell me I'm trespassing and toss me off your ranch."

He laughed. "I'll tell them. Now if you'll come wearing a dress with your hair down, they'll be so dazzled, there's no way they'll mention trespassing. Far from it. We'll all welcome you with open arms."

Smiling, she shook her head. "Nice try, but I don't wear a dress to ride a horse." She shrugged. "In fact, I don't wear a dress anywhere around home. But you can tell them I'm coming."

"Sure. Better yet, let me know beforehand and I'll pick you up. I probably should do that anyway, so they all know we have a truce of sorts." He turned more so that he faced her in his seat. "And it is a truce, Lindsay. Definite and permanent. I'll never again be able to fight with you."

"Don't say things you don't mean, Tony. Your intentions might be good, but there is no way this side of hell that you'll be able to stick by that statement."

Once again he leaned in closer and her heartbeat quickened as it had before. "Yes, there is definitely a way that I can be influenced to stick by that statement. You can wind me around your little finger if you really want to."

"I don't believe that one."

"You should," he said, settling back in his seat again. "Before tonight, did you ever think we would get along as well as we have?"

"Of course not." She tilted her head to study him. "In some ways, we're strangers. There's a lot I don't know about you."

"That's true and a lot I don't know about you. But strangers? No way, Lindsay. There is much I want to explore and discover about you and I intend to do that tonight," he said in a husky voice that made her heartbeat jump again.

Cutting into their conversation, their pilot announced descent into Dallas, and in a short time Lindsay looked out at the twinkling city lights spread far into the distance.

"Do you have your car at the club?" Tony asked.

"No. I left it at the hotel and took a cab."

"Good thinking," he said.

Once they arrived back at the country club, a valet brought Tony's car around and in minutes they drove through the iron gates to his condo complex.

As soon as Lindsay entered his unit, she walked through his entry hall to cross the spacious living room and look out over the sparkling lights of downtown Dallas.

"You have a gorgeous view."

"Do I ever," he said, and she smiled when she turned to see him looking at her.

"I meant the city lights," she explained, knowing he understood exactly what she had referred to.

"Want a drink?" he asked.

"Yes. White wine, please."

He removed his jacket and tie, dropping them on a chair, and walked to a bar in a corner of the room.

"This is a large living area. It's very nice," she said, looking at comfortable brown leather chairs and a long leather sofa.

"It's convenient when I'm here, which is not too often. A few days here and I'm ready for the ranch."

"That I understand," she said, crossing to the bar to perch on a stool and watch him pour her wine.

"I have a full bar if you prefer something else."

"The wine is good."

He handed her the glass and picked up a cold beer. "I figured you for a cold brew," he said, smiling at her.

He set his bottle on the counter, his gaze skimming over her legs when her skirt fell open just above her knees. "Lindsay, it's a crime to hide legs like yours all the time."

"You have no idea what I do all the time. We see each other about once every four or five months at best."

"That I intend to change."

She shook her head. "You know as well as I do that we'll go right back to our usual way of life when the sun rises in the morning."

"I hope to hell not," he said, holding up his bottle of beer in a toast. "Here's to the most beautiful neighbor I'll ever have and to a night I'll never forget."

Laughing softly, she touched his bottle with her wineglass and sipped her wine.

"Here's to the day we can both be civil to each other," she said.

"I'll drink to that." He touched her glass, took a sip of beer and set his bottle on the bar. "But we're going to be much more than civil to each other," he said, the amusement no longer visible in his expression. With his deep blue eyes gazing intently at her, he took her drink from her hand and placed it on the bar. Her heartbeat quickened in anticipation while desire burned in the depths of his eyes.

"I've waited all evening for this moment—to be alone with you," he said, stepping closer. His arm circled her waist and he lifted her off the bar stool easily, standing her on her feet and drawing her into his embrace as his gaze lowered to her mouth.

Desire made her draw a deep breath as he leaned closer, and then she closed her eyes, winding her arms around his neck, surrendering to his kiss.

The moment his mouth settled on hers, her heart slammed against her ribs as passion ignited and desire overwhelmed her. Tony was hard, his chest sculpted with muscles, his biceps like rocks from constant ranch work. She breathed in his scent and knew she would remember it forever. She wound her fingers through his short hair and returned his kiss, wanting to stir him as much as he did her. She tightened her arms around him without having to stand on tiptoe to kiss him because her heels added inches to her height.

As Tony drew her more tightly against him, his warm hand played over her bare back and then up to her shoulders. Dimly she felt him push away her straps as they slipped down on her arms. In seconds she was aware of slight tugs to her scalp when he removed the pins and her hair fell over her shoulders and down on her back.

Slowly, while he kissed her senseless, he drew away each pin until finally her hair framed her face.

He raised his head to look at her, running his fingers slowly through the long locks. "You're so beautiful. You take my breath away, Lindsay," he whispered, sounding as if he meant every word. How could she find this pleasure with Tony? Or want him so desperately?

She had meant this night to be lighthearted, friendly, seductive, so afterward he would be civil to her and try to cooperate with her. She hadn't considered there could be this unbelievable, fiery attraction that he seemed to feel as much as she did.

No matter what he said, they'd go back to their old ways after tonight, though maybe not as contentious. This blazing attraction was for one night only. Tonight she wanted this time with him because she had never before desired or reacted to a man the way she did Tony.

His gaze shifted to her mouth and he leaned down to kiss her again. How long they stood kissing, she didn't know, but at some point, Tony picked her up to carry her to the sofa, switching off the overhead lighting, leaving only the bar light glowing softly.

She planned on some kisses and caresses and then she'd stop. Truthfully, she had never even planned on this much. Dancing, some laughs, a good time, maybe some flirting as she tried to soften him up so he would be more receptive to what she wanted.

She had never dreamed it was possible for Tony's kisses to turn her world upside down, to make her heart-beat race and cause her to desire him more than any other man. She was on fire. As if of their own accord, her hips shifted slightly against him, pressing tightly and feeling his hardness. He was ready for her.

Astounded by the need she felt for him and the re-sponse his kisses evoked in her, she kissed him wildly, her fingers unfastening the studs on his shirt, finally pushing away the fabric. Wanting to touch him, she ran her hands over his warm, rock-hard chest, growing bolder when she heard him take a deep, trembling breath. He set her on her feet while he continued to kiss her.

She felt his fingers at her waist at the back of her dress and then felt him tug down the zipper. He ran his hand lightly over her bottom and she moaned softly as her de-sire intensified.

While he kissed her, his hands slipped lightly up her back and across her shoulders and then came down to push her red dress over her hips so it fell softly around her ankles.

Tony stepped back to look at her. She wore only lacy bikini panties.

His eyes had darkened to a stormy blue-green and he let out a ragged breath. "I'll never forget this moment," he whispered, and stepped to her to crush her against him, kissing her deeply, a kiss that made her feel wanted and

loved. She knew she wasn't loved by him, but he made
her feel that way, as if he needed her more than he had
ever needed any other woman.

He showered kisses on her throat while his hands
cupped her full breasts and his thumbs circled their tips.
His kisses moved lower until his lips met one breast while
his hands caressed the other.

Running her fingers in his hair, she gasped with pleasure when his tongue circled her nipple. She was awash
in desire, wanting him more than she had ever dreamed
possible. She wanted his loving; she wanted all of him.

She had made a decision much earlier to end this night
before it led to lovemaking, and she'd stuck with it even
as they flew back to Dallas. But now desire forced her to
rethink her decision, instinctively feeling that this moment would not come again.

Common sense told her that, come morning, they
would go back, at least partially, to the arguments they
had had all their adult lives. Tonight was special, a once-
in-a-lifetime magical night that would never come again,
and what they did tonight, all their loving, would carry
no ties after dawn.

Tony was incredible. No man had ever excited her the
way he had, and no man would ever make love to her the
way she knew he would. Beyond that, she was unable to
think when his hands and mouth were on her. But she
was able to make a decision. She pulled back and looked
into his eyes.

"Tony, I'm not protected."

He raised his head, kissing her lightly. "I'll take care
of it," he whispered, and leaned down to kiss and fondle
her other breast.

She wanted him with all her being, wanted to make
love with him for the rest of the night. With deliberation

her fingers unfastened his trousers. He grasped her wrist and she paused as he released her to yank off his boots and then his socks. He dropped them carelessly to the floor and returned to kissing her while she pushed down his trousers and then peeled away his briefs.

Her heartbeat raced as her gaze swept over his muscled body. His manhood was thick and hard, ready to love. Stepping closer, she caressed him while he stroked and showered her with kisses.

He picked her up again, kissing her when he carried her through his condo. She clung to him with her eyes closed as they kissed. He touched a light and she glanced quickly to see they were in a bedroom. She returned to kissing him until he stood her on her feet. He reached down to yank away the comforter covering his high, king-size bed.

Watching him, she felt her heart drum in anticipation of the pleasure he would give her. As her gaze swept over his muscled body, she trembled. He stepped back, looking at her in a slow, thorough study that made her tingle as much as if his fingers had moved over her in feathery caresses.

"So beautiful, so perfect," he whispered, drawing her into his embrace as he leaned over her to kiss her hungrily. His hard erection pressed against her, his hard body hot and solid against her.

Why did she want him so desperately and respond to him so intensely? His slightest touch set her quivering and his kisses rocked her, building in her a need unlike she had ever felt before. How could she have found this with Tony?

She couldn't answer her question. Nor did she care. She just wanted Tony and his loving for the rest of the night.

He lifted her into his arms again and placed her on the white sheets, kneeling beside her, his knees lightly pressing against her thighs. Then, as if in a dream—or a fantasy—he rained kisses from her ankles to her mouth.

She writhed, her hips moving slightly as blinding need built inside her until she wanted him more than she ever thought possible.

"Tony, make love to me," she whispered.

"Not so fast, darlin'. We're going to take our time and love for hours," he whispered, still showering her with kisses.

His endearment, spoken in a tender voice that she had never heard before from him, was as effective as his caresses.

"Tony," she gasped, sitting up to grasp his shoulders. "Make love to me. Let me love you."

"Shh, darlin'," he said softly while he kissed her breasts between his words. "Lie down and turn over, let me kiss you," he said, pushing gently.

She rolled onto her stomach and he picked up her foot to kiss her ankle lightly and then brush kisses higher up the back of her leg. He traced circles with his tongue on the back of her knee.

Digging her fingers into the bed, she raised her head slightly to look over her shoulder. "Tony, I can't touch or kiss you this way."

"You will soon," he whispered, and returned to his tender ministrations, trailing his tongue slowly up the back and then along the inside of her thigh.

Aflame with longing, she twisted and rolled over, sitting up to wrap her arms around his neck and kiss him, pouring all her hunger for him into her kiss, wanting to drive him as wild as he had her.

They fell back on the bed with Tony over her, his weight welcome against her. While she moved her hips against him, he kissed her as he rolled beside her. "Do you like me to touch you here?" he whispered, fondling her breast. "Do you want me to kiss you here?" he whispered, moving to brush kisses on her inner thigh, watching her as he did. "You're beautiful."

His words heightened the moment, making her more aware of him and what he was doing while she was lost in sensation and desire.

While he kissed her, his hand trailed up her leg to the inside of her thighs. When he stroked her she gasped with pleasure.

His hand moved against her, driving her to new heights. She didn't think she could take more and she reveled in the feelings he evoked in her. Needing him, she reached out and took him in one hand as her other played over his chest.

She wanted him to feel the same heady sensations he was strumming in her, so she caressed him, eliciting a growl deep in his throat. He stopped her, but he continued to love her, driving her to the brink, lifting her to the precipice of release. And then, when she was about to fall over, he pulled his touch away, shifting his hands to caress her breasts as he also showered them with kisses.

Her fingers wound in his hair. "Tony, I want you. I'm ready," she gasped, moaning with pleasure as he continued to kiss each breast, his tongue drawing lazy circles over each nipple. His fingers dallied on her stomach, but when they slipped lower, she arched against him, thrusting her hips and spreading her legs to give him access.

That was all the urging he needed. Or so she thought. He moved between her legs and she clutched his buttocks, pulling him toward her. "Tony, I want you now," she whispered. But he didn't enter her.

The warm, solid weight of him pressed against her as he stretched over her and kissed her with a hunger that made her heart pound even harder. She wrapped her long legs around him, wanting him more with each second that ticked past. Never before had she wanted to make love as much as she did now.

"Tony," she whispered again, the rest of her words smothered by his mouth covering hers and his tongue entwining with hers.

How could she want him so much? She couldn't answer her own question, she just knew she did. She ached for him, her pulse pounding. "Tony, I can't keep waiting…"

"Yes, you can and it'll be better than ever," he said. He laved her breasts, teasing her nipples between his teeth, and she felt a tug between her legs. All the while, his hands caressed her, binding them in one night of love-making that she would always remember. Though this night could not be repeated, she knew this was the time to make memories she'd carry with her forever.

"I want you now," she finally gasped, tugging him closer.

He stepped off the bed to open a night table drawer and then he watched her, his eyes burning her, as he stood beside the bed to slowly put on the condom.

As she caressed his thigh, her hips shifted slightly in anticipation. She wished he would hurry. Then, he knelt between her legs, his eyes still on hers, as he finally entered her. She wrapped her legs around him again, caressing his smooth, muscled back and hard buttocks, as he slowly thrust into her. She cried out, arching to meet him, wanting him to move with her to give her release for all the tension that coiled tightly in her.

Hot and hard, his manhood filled her, moving slowly, driving her to greater need as she clung to him and moved beneath him in perfect sync.

"Now," she cried, running her hands over his muscled thighs. He obeyed her, and her hips moved faster, her head thrashing as she was lost in the throes of passion, until finally he gave one last thrust, deep and hard, and she cried out. Arching under him, her fingers raking his back, her hips thrusting against him, she found that elusive release and he followed her, bursting within her.

"Tony," she cried.

"Ah, darlin'…" He ground out the words through clenched teeth as his body continued to move over hers.

Finally, satiated, they stilled.

"You're fantastic in every way," he whispered, kissing her temple lightly, trailing light kisses down her cheek and sighing as he lowered his weight carefully onto her.

Gasping for breath, she clung to him while her heartbeat and breathing returned to normal. Tony rolled to his side. He kept her with him, his legs entwined with hers.

"I don't want to let you go."

"You don't have to right now. I want to stay here in your arms, against you. Tony, this has been a wonderful, once-in-a-lifetime night."

"I agree," he said, hugging her lightly and kissing her forehead. "Our lives have changed."

"Not really. It may not ever again be as bad or as hateful, but tonight doesn't really change what we'll face tomorrow. My water problems, you telling me what I should or should not do, not to mention the next thing that'll come up between us."

There was silence while he toyed with locks of her hair. It seemed to her that many minutes went by until he finally spoke. "There's one question I'd like you to answer. Is water what was behind your high bid tonight? You wanted something from me, Lindsay, and I haven't heard one word about what it is."

Three

At his question, she felt her very core stiffen. She didn't want to get into that with him lying beside her and her wrapped in his arms. She didn't want to say anything that would upset him and break the spell that had been woven around them.

"We'll talk about that tomorrow. Tonight is special, Tony. I want to keep it magical until the sun rises and brings the reality of our regular lives back to us. Is that okay with you?"

"Sure, because I have plans for the rest of this magical night. Big plans."

"I do hope they involve me and your sexy body and your wild kisses."

"My sexy body and wild kisses? Wow. Definitely back to my plans for tonight," he said, leaning down to kiss her again. In minutes he propped his head on his hand to look at her again.

She couldn't tell from his eyes what he was thinking. "What?" she asked him.

He toyed with a strand of her hair as he answered. "At this moment I can't imagine ever returning to the way we were. All I'll have to do is remember tonight. All of it, darlin'."

"You better stop calling me darlin' when we go back to real life."

"I can call you that if I want."

"I suspect you won't really want to, but it's very nice tonight under the circumstances."

He smiled at her. "As you said, this is a magical night. One giant surprise after another. And deep down, I know you're right. We'll go back to our ordinary lives and our usual fights, except maybe they won't be quite so bad. After tonight I'll listen, I'll try to cooperate with you and maybe even do what you want."

She couldn't hold back a laugh. "Like hell you will!"

He chuckled, a deep throaty sound that she could feel in her hand as it lay on his muscled chest. Her fingers traced the solid muscles in his shoulders, chest and arms. Occasionally, she would feel the rough line of a scar. His daily outdoor work not only showed in the strength of his fit body but in his scars, as well.

He pulled her close against his side. "Do you have to go home tomorrow? I hope not. I want to stay right here."

"I suppose I don't, until late afternoon. I'll need to be home early Monday morning," she answered, thinking more about his flat stomach, hard with muscles and dusted with hair, over which she ran her fingers.

"Good. I have plans and they involve staying right here and not talking to anyone except each other."

"I have to check out of the hotel tomorrow by noon,

though. That room was paid for by the auction board."
She drew another circle slowly on his stomach.

"I'll call and have tomorrow night put on my card, so
you can get your things whenever you're ready," he said,
rolling over and stretching out his long arm to retrieve
his phone. "What hotel?"

"I can do that."

"Don't argue. We're not going to disagree with each
other this weekend."

She smiled as she told him the name of her hotel and
watched him get the number on his phone. Once again she
thought his take-charge attitude was delightful when he
focused on her. When he finished and she had the room
for another night, he turned to take her into his arms again.

"Thanks, Tony. That was nice of you," she said, running her fingers over the dark stubble on his jaw. "I have
to say, I didn't know I could ever be quite so fascinated
by a cowboy's body."

"I guarantee you, I'm totally fascinated by a cowgirl's
body," he said, trailing his fingers lightly over her breasts.
Even though she had a sheet pulled up over her, she felt
his feathery caresses, and her rapidly heating body responded to them.

"A beautiful blonde cowgirl," he continued, as his eyes
seemed to feast on her. "I want you here with me as long
as possible."

She felt the same way and had no desire to get up and
leave him. Though her heart wished the night could go
on forever, she couldn't get her head around the fact that
she was in Tony Milan's bed. "My family would never
believe we're together tonight. No one would."

"All those people who heard what you paid for a night
with me will believe it."

She laughed. "I suppose you're right." She rolled over

and sat up slightly to look down at him. "You're really amazing, you know that? Tonight is astonishing. I never dreamed it would be like this."

"I promise you that I didn't, either." His face took on a sheepish look. "When I stepped out on that auction stage earlier, I didn't really think anyone would bid for me."

"Now that is ridiculous."

"I'm just a cowboy."

"A cowboy named Milan—a name that's well known in these parts. And a very wealthy rancher," she remarked. "With all the ranches and businesses owned by your family, I think you could count on someone bidding for an evening with you."

"Who bid against you? I couldn't see either one of you because of the lights in my eyes, not until you stood to come to the stage and a spotlight picked you out. As soon as I laid eyes on you, my attitude about the evening did an immediate reversal."

She smiled at him. "I don't know who bid against me. There were people from Dallas and Lubbock there, and from other places, as well. Probably one of your old girlfriends who wasn't ready to say goodbye," she said.

"Let's not discuss my old girlfriends," he said through a grin. "I'd much rather talk about you anyway. I still say if you'd wear a dress to town, you'd have a slew of guys asking you out."

"I don't want a 'slew' of locals asking me out, thank you very much."

"Why not? There are nice guys out there."

"Sure there are, but they're ranchers and cowboys. I don't want to go out with ranchers or cowboys."

"You could've fooled me. You paid a small fortune to go out with a rancher tonight, in case you've forgotten."

"I won't ever forget you," she said, hoping she kept

her voice light, but a shiver slithered down her spine because she suspected she had spoken the absolute truth. This had turned into the best night of her life because of Tony. He'd charmed her, seduced her and become the most appealing man she had ever known—as long as she didn't think about him as a rancher.

He didn't let the subject drop. Instead, he questioned her. "Why don't you want to go out with ranchers or cowboys? We're nice guys."

"I know you guys are nice. It's just that—" She stopped, hesitating to tell him the truth. But Tony deserved an answer to his question. "I'm a ranch owner, remember? I'm not a party girl out for fun. I'm also not a sweetie who'll go dancing and come home and cook and have a family and kiss a cowboy goodbye every morning while he goes out to work and listen politely to him at night while he tells me bits and pieces about what he had to do at work. Even worse, I don't want to fall for another rancher and have him tell me how to run my ranch."

"I should have guessed. Two bosses can't run a ranch."

"Not my ranch," she said.

"If you don't marry a rancher or a cowboy, the guy is going to want to move you to the city."

"Now you're beginning to get the picture—the complete picture—of why I never wear dresses. I can't imagine marrying a city guy, either, so there you are." She gave a nod of her head, then shrugged. "I have a nice life. I have my nephew, Scotty, who stays with me a lot, and soon there will be another baby in Mike's family."

"But, Lindsay, you were meant for marriage in so many ways. I hope some guy comes along and sweeps you off your feet and you can't say no. Rancher or city guy."

She giggled. "My, oh, my. Is this a sideways proposal?"

He grinned. "You know better than that. We're doing

well together tonight, but for a lifetime…? Would you want that?"

She studied him, knowing she had to make light of his question, but another shiver ran down her spine and she couldn't explain why. She squeezed his biceps. "Mmm, you do make good husband material. You have all your teeth and they look in good shape and you're healthy and strong and light on your feet. And you're incredibly sexy." She gave an exaggerated sigh. "Given our past and probably our future, I think I have to answer…no."

"Incredibly sexy? Oh, darlin', come here." He drew her closer, but she resisted and placed her hand against his chest.

"Whoa, cowboy. Don't let that compliment go to your head…or other parts," she said, and he grinned.

"I told you our future will not be like our past."

She had to agree. "I don't think it will, either."

"Right now I want to relish the present. How about a soak in the tub?"

"A splendid idea," she said, already eager to be naked in the water with him.

He stood and picked her up. She yelped in surprise as she slid her arm around his neck. "I never dreamed you could be so much fun or so charming."

"I promise you, I have to say the same about you. And, to boot, you're breathtakingly beautiful and hot and sexy. I guarantee that sentiment will not end when morning comes," he added with an intent look that made her heart skip a beat.

He carried her to a huge two-room bathroom. One room held plants, mirrors, two chaise longues with a glass-topped iron table between them, plus dressing tables, a shower and an oversize sunken Jacuzzi tub.

Soon they were soaking in a tub of swirling hot water while she sat between his legs, leaning back against him.

"Tony, this is decadent. It feels wonderful."

"I suspect you're referring to the hot water and not my naked body pressed against yours. Right?"

"I won't answer that question."

"An even better choice than I expected from you. Also, I seem to remember a short time ago hearing you say something about my sexy body and wild kisses," he whispered, fondling her breasts as he kissed her nape.

"That I did and I meant it," she concurred, running her hands over his strong legs.

In no time, desire overwhelmed her, and their playful moment transformed. She turned to sit astride him. Placing her hands on both sides of his face, she leaned forward to kiss him, long and thoroughly, her hair falling over his shoulders. He was ready to love her again, too—she felt it. His hands caressed her breasts, then slid down over her torso to her inner thigh. His fingers glided higher, stroking her intimately until she closed her eyes and clung to him, her hips moving as he loved her.

"Tony, you need protection," she said, her eyes flying open.

"So I do," he said, reaching behind him for his terry robe on the footstool. He took a condom out of the pocket and, in seconds, he was sheathed and ready. He pulled her close again, lifting her so he could enter her in one smooth stroke. She locked her legs around him and lowered herself onto his hard shaft.

Her climax came fast, as if they hadn't made love earlier, and she achieved another before Tony reached his. When he was sated, he watched her with hooded eyes and she wondered what he thought.

She picked up a towel to dry herself, her gaze running

over broad shoulders that glistened with drops of water.
"I'll see you in bed," she said, leaning close to kiss him.
His arm snaked out to wrap around her neck.

"I want to keep you right here in my arms," he said
between kisses. Damp locks of his hair clung to his forehead and he felt warm and wet.

"I'll see you in bed," she repeated with amusement.
"You're insatiable. When do you run out of energy?"

"With you, I hope never."

She laughed, snatching up another towel to wrap
around herself as she got out of the tub and headed to bed.

She felt as if she was having an out-of-body experience. The night continued to shock her—Tony continued
to shock her. She couldn't believe he'd given her the best
sex of her life, three bone-shattering orgasms—and the
night wasn't over yet.

She walked into a big closet and looked at his clothes
so neatly hanging. Boots were lined in rows. She found
what she wanted—a navy terry robe—and she pulled it
on, belting it around her waist.

She climbed into bed, detecting a faint scent of Tony's
aftershave, wondering how long it would be before he
joined her.

In minutes he walked through the door and her heart
skipped a beat. With a navy towel knotted around his
waist, he oozed sex appeal as he crossed the room.

"I couldn't wait to be with you. You look more gorgeous than ever," he said, discarding his towel and scooting beneath the sheet. "Want a drink? Something to eat?
Music and dancing?"

She laughed out loud. "You've got to be kidding.
Relax, Tony. Sit back and enjoy the moment." She sobered
and ran her fingers over his smooth jaw. "You shaved."

"Just for you." Turning on his side, he pulled her close against him. "This is better. I like your hair down best."

"I rarely wear it that way, but I'll keep that in mind."

"No, you won't. You'll forget." He ran his fingers through the damp locks. "You know you never gave me an answer to my invitation to go to dinner next Friday night."

She was silent, mulling over his question. She had wanted to accept instantly when he had asked her the first time, but reluctance had filled her. It still did. "I think when we go back to our real lives, you'll wish you hadn't asked me."

"Not so."

"Call me next week and ask me again if you still want to go out. I don't think you will."

"Darlin', if I didn't want you to go, I wouldn't ask you."

"Just call me next week."

He gave her a long look and she wondered what was running through his mind. Had their mild clash reminded him of the big fights they'd had? From the shuttered look that had come to his eyes, she suspected it had. She didn't want any such intrusion on this night. She scooted close against him. "In the meantime, I intend to keep you happy with me," she said, hoping for a sultry voice.

The shuttered look was replaced by blatant desire, and she guessed she had succeeded in making things right between them again. When he turned to kiss her, she was certain she had.

It was midafternoon the next day when she walked out of the shower. Wearing the navy robe again, she roamed through his sprawling condo into a big kitchen that had an adjoining sitting room with a fireplace.

Exploring the refrigerator and his freezer, she saw

some drinks, a few covered dishes and an assortment of berries. She had leaned down to look at the lower shelves when Tony's arms circled her waist to draw her back against him. He nuzzled her neck.

"I know what I want," he said.

She turned to wrap her arms around his neck. He wore another thick navy robe that fell open over his broad chest.

Aware their idyll was about to end, she kissed him passionately. She dreaded stepping back into reality, where she would have to wrangle with him again.

He released her. "Hold that thought and let me put something in the oven so I can feed us."

"At last…food," she said, clutching her heart and batting her eyelashes dramatically at him. When she licked her lips slowly as she watched him remove the covered casserole dish from the fridge and nudge the door closed, he placed the dish on the counter and turned to draw her into his arms.

"You were going to get fed until you did that," he said in a husky voice, pulling her close.

"Did what?"

"You know what," he said, leaning closer to kiss her, a hungry kiss that ignited fires more swiftly than ever.

In minutes she wriggled out of his grasp. "I think we should eat. Whatever I did, I won't do again. How can I help?"

He was breathing hard, looking down, and she realized the top of her robe was pulled apart enough to reveal her breasts. She closed the robe more tightly. "As I was saying, what can I do to help?"

He seemed to not even hear her, but in seconds he looked up. "If you want to eat, I suggest you go sit over there on the sofa and talk to me while I get something heated up. If you stay within arm's reach, I'm reaching."

She smiled and left him alone, watching him put the dish into the oven and get plates, pour juice, wash berries. Her gaze raked over him. He was a gorgeous man. Sexy, strong, successful. Why hadn't some woman snatched him up already? As far as she knew from local gossip, there had never been a long-term girlfriend. Just a trail of girlfriends who'd come and gone. Apparently, he didn't go in for serious affairs.

"Tony, you really should let me help you. I feel silly sitting here doing nothing except watching you work."

"This isn't hard work. You stay where you are so I'm not too distracted to get breakfast on the table."

"I do that to you? Distract you?"

"Lindsay," he said in a threatening tone, "do you want breakfast or do you want to go back to bed?"

She laughed. "Breakfast. I'm famished. And I'll help any way I can."

"You know what you can do, so do it," he said.

"Yes, sir," she answered demurely, teasing him. When his gaze raked over her, she became aware of the top of her robe gaping open enough to give a another glimpse of her breasts and the lower half of her robe falling open over her crossed legs. She closed her robe and belted it tightly, glancing up to find him still watching her.

"Show's over," she said.

He nodded and turned to finish preparing the meal.

After a breakfast of egg-and-bacon casserole and fruit, he turned on music as they cleared the table, and took her wrist. "Stop working and come dance with me," he said, moving to a familiar lively rock number.

Unable to resist him, she danced with him, aware as

she did that her robe gaped below her waist, revealing her legs all the way to her thighs.

Next a ballad came on and he drew her into his arms to slow dance. He was aroused, ready to make love again. His arms tightened around her and he shifted closer to kiss her. Dimly she was aware they had stopped dancing.

His hand trailed down between them to untie her robe while he continued kissing her. When she reached out to do the same, his belt was tightly knotted and she needed his help, but soon both robes were open. He shoved them aside, pulling her naked body against his.

Her soft moan was a mixture of pleasure and desire as he kissed her and picked her up to carry her back to bed.

It was almost two hours later when he held her close beside him in bed and rolled over to look at her. He wound his fingers in the long strands of her hair, toying with her locks.

"I know you have to go home soon," he said. "I think it's time we get to the reason behind this weekend and your incredible bid for me at the auction. You paid a mind-boggling sum to get my attention, so now you have it. What's behind this? What did you want me to agree to do?"

Tony looked into her big eyes that were the color of blue crystal. His gaze went to her mouth and he wanted to kiss her again. He stifled the urge, difficult as it was. Their time together had been fabulous, a dream, but it would end shortly and they would go back to their regular lives. How much would it change because of the auction? For a moment a memory flashed in his mind of the second and most direct encounter they had, when a big tree on her property fell during a storm in the night. It had fallen on his fence, taking it down and also smashing one of his trucks, which had stalled in the rainstorm.

One of the men had called to tell him. When he drove out to view the damage, she was already there with a crew working to cut up the fallen tree and haul it away. She held a chain saw and had a battered straw hat on her head with a long braid hanging over her shoulder. He'd known her all his life but rarely paid any attention to her. He knew she was two years younger than he was, but right then he thought she looked five years younger. The noise of chain saws was loud, the ground spongy from the rain when he stepped out of his truck.

Even though she had to pay for the damage because it was her tree, he'd tried to curb his anger that she hadn't called him first. She saw him and walked over.

"My tree fell in the storm. Sorry about the damage. But I'm insured."

"Did you call your agent?"

"No, I will. I want to get the fence up as soon as possible so I don't lose any livestock."

"Lindsay, that's my fence and I'll fix it. You should have called me. Your insurance should cover the damages when a tree falls on something, but only if you have notified your company. They would have sent someone out to see what happened, take pictures and write a report. Now the tree is back on your property, cut up as we speak, and I doubt if you can collect anything."

She had looked surprised. "I haven't had a tree fall on anything before. I'll check with my insurance company, and I'll pay you for the damage."

"Stop cutting up the tree. I'm going to call and see if my adjustor wants to come out anyway."

She'd frowned but agreed.

"And leave the fence alone. It's my fence and I'll get it replaced today."

She had scowled at him. "Today?"

"This morning," he said. "As soon as we can. If you have livestock grazing here, move them. Don't let them in this pasture. That's simple enough," he said, wondering if she knew how to run that ranch of hers.

"I know that," she snapped.

"Leave the fence to me. Stop cutting up and hauling away the tree. I'll get someone out here to look this over," he repeated, suspecting she was stubborn enough to keep cutting up the tree.

She had clamped her mouth closed as her blue eyes flashed. "Anything else you want to tell me to do?" she snapped, and his temper rose a notch.

"Probably a lot, but I'm not going to," he answered evenly.

"Why was your truck parked right by my property?"

He had been annoyed by her question, though he tried to hang on to his temper. "It was on my property and we can park the truck wherever we want on this side of that fence. If you want to know, one of the men was headed back in the storm and checking to see if the fences were okay. He'd been driving through high water in several low places and the truck quit running here. Unfortunately, near your tree."

She'd been silent a moment as if thinking about what he had said. "I know it was my tree on your truck. My word should be good enough for the insurance."

Impatiently, he shook his head. "No, it's not good enough. Next time, remember to call your adjustor before you do anything else. You may have a hard time collecting."

He remembered her raising her chin defiantly and he'd

wondered if she would argue, but then she looked around and seemed lost in thought until she turned back to him. "That isn't a new truck. Get three estimates in Verity for the repairs and I'll cover the lowest bidder's charges."

"Look, I can't get that kind of damage fixed in Verity. At least not at three different places and you know it. The truck will be totaled."

"I'm not buying you a brand-new truck."

"Tell your guys to stop working and then go home, Lindsay, and call your insurance company. They'll tell you what to do next."

Her cheeks had grown red and fire had flashed in her eyes, but he hadn't cared if his instructions made her angry. She had already annoyed the hell out of him.

Yes, Lindsay Calhoun had that unique ability to boil his blood.

Right now, though, as he reined his thoughts back to the present and looked down at her naked body, she had the ability to heat his blood in a different way.

Tony pushed aside the past to gaze into her big blue eyes. He didn't expect what they'd had this weekend to last much longer because the real world was settling back into their lives.

Last night he hadn't cared what she wanted from him. He'd been totally focused on her as he adjusted to his new discoveries about her. Now, though, curiosity reared its ugly head and he wanted to learn her purpose behind the evening.

"You should know what I want to talk about," she said, scooting to sit up in bed and lean back against pillows, pulling the sheet demurely high and tucking it beneath her arms. Her pale yellow hair spilled over her shoulders. She looked tousled, warm and soft, and he wanted to wrap his arms around her and kiss her again, but he refrained. It was time he heard her out and learned what was so important to her that she would pay several thousand dollars just to get his attention.

"Two things, Tony," she said, and he sighed, trying to be quiet and listen, to be patient and talk to her calmly. He had already given her the solution to her water problem, but she didn't believe him. He could deal with this in a civilized manner, but underneath all her sex appeal, breathtaking beauty and their dream weekend, there still was the real woman who was mule-stubborn and did not take advice well.

Lindsay was all he avoided in women—stubborn, far too serious and constantly stirring conflict.

The irony of the fact that she was now sharing his bed was not lost on him. But he ignored it as he focused on her.

She continued her explanation. "First and foremost I hope that we have some sort of truce where we can be civil to each other, with no tempers flaring."

"I'd say we can be mighty civil to each other. You should have some of your money's worth there," he said, caressing her throat, letting his fingers drift down lightly over her breast.

"I hope so," she said solemnly.

"I'm willing," he said. "So continue."

She squared her shoulders and fussed with the sheet. Then she cleared her throat and spoke. "My wells are running dry and I figured you've replaced your old pumps with bigger ones that are drawing on the aquifer and depleting my groundwater. I can get bigger pumps, too, but that might take water from other neighbors and I don't want to do that."

He held up his hand. "I told you, Lindsay, I do not have bigger pumps."

"Well, for some reason, my water is dwindling away to almost nothing."

"It's a record drought," he said, as if having to explain the obvious to a child.

"I've asked Cal Thompson and he doesn't have bigger pumps. Neither does Wendell Holmes. I figured it was you."

"It is not. According to the weather experts, this is the worst drought in these parts in the past almost sixty years—before you and I were born, much less before we became owners of neighboring ranches. I told you the solution to my problem. You can do the same. Just dig deeper wells and you'll have much more water. Then when it rains, the aquifer will fill back up again. If you don't want to dig deeper, buy water and have it piped in. That's what Wendell is doing."

She stared at him thoughtfully in silence for several minutes. It was difficult to keep his attention on her water worries while she sat beside him in bed, naked, with only a sheet pulled up beneath her arms. He couldn't resist reaching out to caress her throat again, letting his hand slide down and slip beneath the sheet to caress her bare breasts. It took an effort to sit quietly and wait when all he wanted to do was take her in his arms and kiss her thoroughly. Well, that wasn't all he wanted to do.

The instant his fingers brushed her nipple, he saw a flicker in her eyes.

"You really had them dug deeper?"

Thinking more about her soft skin and where his fingers wanted to go, he hung on to his patience. "Yes, I did. When we get home, come over anytime and I'll show you my old pumps."

When she merely nodded, he felt a streak of impatience with her for being so stubborn. She didn't seem convinced he was telling the truth, and he suspected she wasn't going to take his advice. With every passing minute he could see her sliding back into her serious, stubborn self, stirring up conflict unnecessarily. Lindsay seemed to thrive on conflict. Except for last night. For that brief time she had been sexy, appealing, cooperative and wonderful. Now they were drifting back to reality and he had to hang on to his patience once again.

"I might do that."

As his gaze ran over her, it was difficult to think about anything else except how sexy she was and how the minutes were running out on this brief truce. She looked incredibly enticing with her bare shoulders and just the beginning of luscious curves revealed above the top of the sheet. How could she be this appealing and he had never noticed? He knew his answer, but it still amazed him that he hadn't had a clue about her beauty. In the past, once she started arguing he couldn't see beyond his anger. He saw now.

He was unable to resist trailing his fingers lightly over her alluring bare shoulder, looking so soft and smooth. If his life depended on it, he couldn't stop touching her or looking at her. He wanted to pull away the sheet, place her in his lap and kiss her senseless. They were wasting their last few moments together talking about the drought, when he had other things he wanted to do.

He leaned forward to brush a kiss on that perfect shoulder.

"Tony, you're not even listening," she snapped, her voice taking on the stubborn note he had heard her use too many times. Right now, he didn't care, because he knew how to end her annoyance.

He trailed kisses to her throat and up to her ear while his hands traveled over her, pulling the sheet down as they set out in exploration. Suddenly, she pushed him down and moved over him to sit astride him. She had tossed aside the sheet completely and was naked. It still startled him to realize what a sexy body she had.

"This weekend has opened possibilities I never thought of when I was bidding," she said in a throaty voice while her hands played over his chest.

He cupped her full breasts, their softness sending his temperature soaring. He was fully aroused, hard and ready and wanting her as if they hadn't made love ever.

"I'll leave you with memories that will torment you," she whispered, leaning down to shower kisses over his chest.

He sighed as she moved down his body, her hand stroking his thick rod as she trailed kisses over his abdomen and lower. When she reached his erection, he groaned.

He relished her ministrations, but he didn't want their last time to be like this. He wanted to be inside her. In one smooth motion he rolled her over so he was on top. His mouth covered hers in a demanding, possessive kiss at the same time that he grabbed a condom from the bedside table.

In seconds he entered her, taking her hard and fast while she locked her legs around him and rocked wildly against him in return.

He wanted to bring her to more than one climax, as he'd done before, but this time was too unbridled, too untamed. The second he sent her flying over the edge of an orgasm, he joined her, reaching the stars together on a hell of a ride.

When they slowed and their breathing became regular, he stayed inside her, too exhausted to move. Finally he kissed her lips and said softly, "You can't imagine how beautiful and sexy I think you are."

A smile lit up her eyes, though it did not grace her mouth. "I hope so. I don't want you to forget this weekend," she whispered.

He gazed into her eyes and doubted if he ever would.

This time with her had been special, but now they would be going back to their real lives. While they should be more neighborly in the future, they were still the same people, with the same personalities. Lindsay was not his type—she was way too serious for him and far too stubborn. He suspected today would be goodbye.

He pulled out of her and rolled over.

"I should get ready to go home," she said.

He turned to her. "I'll fly you home if you want to have someone pick up your car. Or I can take you home when I go."

She shook her head. "Thank you, but I'll drive home. I'd better get in the shower now. It's time," she said.

He caught her arm and she pulled up a sheet to cover herself while she paused getting out of bed.

"Lindsay, more water is a poor return on your money. For your bid and for this weekend, you should get a whole lake of water in return."

To his surprise she smiled, standing to wrap the sheet around herself in toga fashion. She walked to the other side of the bed to put her arms around his neck. When she did, he placed his hands on her tiny waist, wanting to kiss her instead of listening to whatever she had to say.

"Maybe not such a poor return," she said in the throaty voice that conjured up images of them in bed together. "We've made some inroads on our fighting that will make a huge change in our relationship. At least the fights in the future might not be so bitter."

He grinned. "We'll see how long we can both hold on to our tempers. All I have to do is remember you like this," he said, leaning down to kiss her lightly as he ran his hands over her back.

"I need to shower," she said, stepping away from him.

"Shucks. I hoped I was irresistible," he drawled, and she smiled.

"You are, Tony. Far too much," she said as she walked away from him, picking up the navy bathrobe on her way to the shower.

After her last statement he was tempted to catch up with her and kiss her again. He wanted to hold her, to see how truly irresistible he could be. But they were getting ready to go home and return to their regular lives and there would be no lovemaking in their future. With a sigh he pulled out some fresh clothes and went down the hall to another bathroom.

All the time she showered, Lindsay wondered how much this weekend would change how they treated each other at home. Tony was still Tony, telling her what to do. She hadn't said anything to him, but she wanted to check his pumps by herself. She wouldn't put it past him to be bluffing with his invitation to come look. After all, he was a Milan.

One of her earliest memories had been her grandmother telling her to never trust a Milan. Could she trust Tony now?

The Tony she had just been with for the past twenty hours was a man she would trust with her life. That thought startled her; it was completely at odds with how she'd been raised. Then again… Had her grandmother just been passing down family opinions that could have gone back generations?

Thirty minutes later, dressed and ready to go, Lindsay joined Tony in the living room. He came to his feet when she entered, his gaze sweeping over her, making her tingle. To her surprise, reluctance to see the weekend end filled her. After all, she and Tony had always known it wouldn't—couldn't—last.

Even in jeans, boots and a navy Western shirt, Tony looked sexy and handsome. A short while ago, as they'd talked about ranching, she'd felt the old annoyance with him for telling her what she should do. Now, simply looking at him made her heart beat faster.

She looked down at the red dress she'd worn last night and wore again now. "I have to go back to my hotel in this. It's four in the afternoon, so I may turn heads," she said, forcing a grin that never made it fully to her lips.

He crossed the room to place his hands on her shoulders. "Lindsay, in that dress, you'll turn heads any hour of the day or night. You're gorgeous." He reached out to play with her hair, which fell about her shoulders. "I like your hair down."

For some reason she hadn't put it up when she got ready. She couldn't say why.

"Thank you. I'm ready to go. You know what the drive is like back to the ranch. Are you going home today?" She knew he was driving her to her hotel, but wasn't sure where he was headed after that.

"No, I have an appointment in Dallas in the morning. Otherwise, I would have pushed harder to go home together."

"I see." She gave one nod. "Well, now we go back to our real lives and the real world. But it was a wonderful, magical weekend that I never, ever expected."

"My sentiments exactly," he said. "I don't want you

to go. I don't want this to end, but I know it has to and it won't be the same."

"Afraid not," she agreed with him. "I'm ready. Shall we go?"

"Yes. But how about one last kiss?" He took her in his arms and he kissed her, hard, as if his kiss was sealing a bond that had been established between them this weekend. His lips were making sure that she would never forget his lovemaking, even though she knew it wouldn't happen again.

She kissed him in kind, wanting just as much to make certain he couldn't forget her, either.

He raised his head. "How about a picture of the two of us to commemorate the occasion?" he asked, pulling out his phone. "Do you know how few selfies I've taken? I think one—with a friend and my horse at a rodeo."

She laughed. "I rank right up there with your horse. Wow."

He grinned as he held out the phone and took the shot, then he showed it to her. "You're gorgeous, Lindsay."

"Look at that picture the next time you think about dumping trash on the entrance to my ranch."

He shook his head. "I'm still telling you that I did not do any such thing. You might have annoyed someone else, you know."

Startled, she studied him. "You really mean that?"

"I really mean it."

"If you didn't do it, then I owe you an apology," she said, still staring at him. But, even if she had accused him of something he didn't do, there was bound to have been things he did do. And he still had those take-charge ways that drove her nuts. Besides, he liked to play the field and never get serious. No, Tony was not for her.

"One picture, Lindsay, just of you, so I can look and

remember. Okay?" he asked, stepping away and taking her picture as she placed her hand on her hip and smiled.

"We have to go. I need to get home," she said, shouldering a delicate, jeweled purse that matched the straps on her dress.

"Sure thing," he said, taking her arm to walk her out to the car. As she slid onto the passenger seat, her skirt fell open and she glanced up to see him looking at her legs. She tucked her skirt around her while he closed the door and walked around to his side of the car.

He was quiet on the ride to the hotel, and so was she. As he drew up to the front entrance a short while later, he stepped out and talked to a valet, then came around to escort her into the lobby. "I'm glad you were the high bidder. But I don't want to say goodbye."

"We both know the weekend is over. Really over. Reality sets in now, Tony. As we've already agreed, it might be a little better than it was."

He nodded. "You take care."

"You, too. Thanks for a weekend that was worth my bid."

"That'll go to my head. I didn't dream I could bring such a price." He smiled as he stepped away. "Goodbye," he said, turning and walking out of the hotel.

She stood watching him, unable to understand the feelings of sadness and loss as he walked away.

Four

When he vanished from sight, she turned to go to her room to change to jeans and get her things to drive back to her real life at her ranch. She wished she had gotten a selfie for herself and then she laughed at herself. If she had, at the first ornery thing he did, she would have erased it. And she didn't expect one weekend to change Tony's alpha-male ways or his flitting from woman to woman.

Even if he changed, which couldn't happen, she didn't care to break her rule about avoiding entanglements with cowboys and ranchers. Tony would be the last man on earth she would want to fall in love with because it would be disaster for each of them from the first minute. They were both ranchers, with clear ideas of how they wanted to run things and opposing ideas on most everything. Life with Tony would be a continual battle. Unless he retired and just stayed in the bedroom. That thought made her laugh out loud as she drove all alone in her car, heading west out of Dallas and back to her ranch.

Midmorning on Tuesday as Tony sat at his ranch desk and worked at his computer, trying to find Texas water sources, his phone rang and he answered to hear his brother Wyatt.

"I thought I better call and see if you survived Saturday night. I heard you didn't come home until Monday evening."

"Keane, my foreman, always knows how to get hold of me. You didn't know I was worth so much money, did you?" Tony asked.

Wyatt laughed. "You brought in a fortune at the auction. And it was all for a good cause, so thanks. You really contributed, but don't let it go to your head. Even though this is bound to bring another slew of admiring females into your life."

Tony hadn't thought of that. "Maybe, but there's one thing I do know. I will never bet with you on saddle bronc riding events again."

Wyatt gave a belly laugh. "How'd the date with Lindsay go, bro? I was worried what she might want to do with you. I gotta tell you, I had no idea she could look like she did."

Tony recalled the blonde beauty who was such a surprise. "Lindsay's looks sent me into shock, and once I caught sight of that red dress, the evening instantly improved. But you shouldn't worry. We did fine together."

"I figured her looks would smooth things over. Don't know if you know yet, but the two of you are all the gossip in Verity and in the sheriff's office. I've been asked more than a few questions. I think around my office, they're waiting for a report from me about how the evening went."

"Civilized. That's what you tell them. We just set aside our differences—for charity."

"I'll bet you did," Wyatt said, and Tony could hear the amusement in his brother's voice. "No way in hell would you fight with someone who looked like she did Saturday night. And she must have wanted something from you badly to pay that kind of money."

"Yeah, she wants more water."

"Don't we all. She should know you can't help her out there. No rain in the forecast, either. Hang on a sec, Tony." Wyatt put him on hold while he consulted with one of his deputies. When he returned, he was back on what appeared to be his favorite subject. "Like I was saying, some people will never look at Lindsay the same way. Those who didn't see her at the auction are curious as hell. I don't know why she keeps those looks hidden."

"She's not interested in dating cowboys or ranchers. She doesn't want anyone telling her how to run her ranch. You can figure that one out."

"Definitely. I was shocked to see who had won the bid," Wyatt remarked drily.

Tony would agree with that. "We had a good time Saturday night, but she's still Lindsay, all stubborn and serious. But we did agree to ease off the fights from now on."

"Thank heaven for that one. My life will get a hell of a lot more peaceful. Call when you come to town."

"Sure, Wyatt."

After he hung up, he stared at the phone, thinking about Lindsay, and he was tempted to pick up the phone and call her. Then reason reared its head. Beneath all that beauty, he reminded himself, she was still the stubborn, obstreperous woman she had always been. She was as wise to avoid ranchers as they were to avoid her. She was not his type. Still…that weekend with her had been the sexiest in his life, and she had been the sexiest woman he'd ever been with.

He had to shake his head to get rid of the images that flooded his mind. The two of them in bed, in the Jacuzzi… No, he had to leave things alone. The weekend was over and it wouldn't happen again.

Breathing a sigh, he turned to the ledger he needed to work on and tried to forget her and the steamy memories of their weekend.

The next few days slipped by without a cloud in the bight blue sky, the drought growing more severe as water dwindled in the creeks and riverbeds and strong, hot winds warmed the parched earth. Lindsay threw herself into work, trying to forget the weekend with Tony, but she was unable to do so. It surprised her how much she thought about him. Even worse, she finally admitted to herself that she missed seeing him. She gritted her teeth at the thought. She didn't want to miss Tony. She didn't want him or the weekend they'd had to be important. Her reactions to him continually shocked her.

All her adult life she had avoided going out with men who would want to tell her how to run her ranch. She had managed, until Tony. That was the road straight to disaster. She didn't want to marry a take-charge male— and a Milan, to boot!—and then fight over running everything. There was no way she would be in agreement on everything or turn her ranch over to someone else to run. She shook her head, knowing she needn't worry. Tony wouldn't ever get close to proposing to her. He wasn't going to propose to any woman. He was not even the type of person she wanted to go out with again, and she was certain he felt the same way about her.

It was done. They were done. It was that simple.

Turning back to work, she forced him out of her mind. Soon she wouldn't even think about him.

But that resolve didn't stop her from mulling over his property. That afternoon when she drove her pickup along the boundary between her ranch and Tony's, she stopped, switched off the engine, got binoculars and climbed up on her pickup to find out if she was close enough to see his pump on the water well nearest her land.

It was visible in the distance, but she couldn't tell whether it was old or new. Damn. Time was running out for her.

How much longer could she go without rain?

Her other neighbors were buying water and having it piped or shipped in.

Tony had told her to come look at his pumps. If he still had the old pumps and he had dug deeper—if he was telling the truth—then that would be the best thing for her to do. She frowned. Why did it rankle so much to do what he told her to do?

As she looked at his land, she couldn't keep from moving her binoculars in a wide swing, curious whether Tony worked in the area. She didn't see him and she hated to admit to herself that she was disappointed. She missed his company. Now she was sorry she hadn't accepted his dinner invitation for Friday night, instead telling him to call her this week if he still wanted to take her out again. She hadn't expected to hear from him and so far, she had been right. It was Thursday and he hadn't called, so he must have had second thoughts when he got home.

She hated to admit that she was disappointed, but she told herself it was for the best. Still, she couldn't stop the memories... She remembered being in his arms, his kisses, his blue-green eyes that darkened to the color of a stormy sea when he was in the throes of passion. How could he be so handsome and so sexy? Maybe it had been the tux. Or his naked body that was male perfection. Or his—

Her ringing phone cut off that steamy train of thought. Shaking her head as she wiped her brow, she yanked her cell out of her pocket expecting Abe, her foreman, but the caller ID read T. Milan. Her heart missed a beat as she stared at the phone until the next ring jolted her out of her surprise. She said hello and heard Tony's deep voice.

"How are you?" he asked politely, and suddenly she was suspicious of why he was calling, but at the same time, she was happy to hear his voice.

"I'm fine. Actually, I'm at our boundary line and looking at your closest well trying to see your pump."

"Hey, are you really? I'm not far. Stay where you are and I'll join you and give you a closer look."

She laughed. "You don't need to."

"Of course I don't need to, but I'm already headed that way, so don't drive off."

"I wouldn't think of it."

"Oh, I almost forgot. I called to ask about dinner tomorrow night."

So he hadn't had second thoughts after all. She couldn't stop the smile from spreading across her lips.

"How about something simpler than last weekend?" he continued before he had her answer. "Like Marty's Roadhouse? I know it's two counties away, but if we go anywhere around here, you'll be besieged by cowboys wanting to take you out. Also, we'll be the top of the list for local gossip."

"I don't want either to happen."

"We'll do a little two-steppin' and eat some barbecue and discuss what you can do to get water."

She should say no. They could talk about water on the phone or when he arrived in a few minutes. Common sense told her to decline. But then she thought about dancing with him. If she just had some self-discipline and had him bring her home after dinner, an evening with him couldn't hurt. "That would be good," she said.

"Great. I'll pick you up at six. We'll have a good time dancing."

She heard a motor. "I think I hear you approaching."

"You do. Stay where you are."

"See you in seconds," she said, and broke the connection. Amused, she pulled on leather gloves and parted strands of barbed wire that formed the fence that divided their property. She had been climbing through or over barbed wire since she was little. She straightened to watch him approach.

He drove up in a red pickup, stopped and jumped down. As he came into view, she saw that he wore a light blue long-sleeved shirt with the sleeves rolled up, tight jeans, boots and a black broad-brimmed hat.

She knew she was going against good sense getting involved any more deeply with Tony. So why did her entire body tingle at the sight of him?

"You look great," Tony said as he approached her and reached out to tug her braid. "I never realized how good you look in jeans."

She laughed. "Until last weekend, I never realized you could look at me without getting annoyed."

Grinning, his gaze roamed down her legs again and every inch of her felt his eyes on her. "Oh, darlin', those jeans do fit you. I just should have taken a second look." He looked into her eyes and her breath caught. How could he cause such a reaction in her now? She had known him all her life and until last weekend she'd never once had this kind of response to him just saying hello.

"I'm glad you said yes to tomorrow night," he said, the amusement fading from his expression.

Her smile vanished when his did. "Tony, we're probably doing something we shouldn't. You and I have no future with each other in a social way."

He didn't argue with her and, instead, continued to stare at her. He shrugged and stepped closer to run his finger along her cheek. The feathery touch sizzled and she had to draw a deep breath and resist walking into his arms.

"It's just a fun Friday night, Lindsay. Surely we can do that just one more time."

She knew the more time she spent with him, the more she could get hurt. Tony would not change, and neither would she. At the next problem to come up between them, he would be telling her what to do and she would be angry with him all over again. She needed to stay rooted in reality for the good of her ranch, because she couldn't afford to be sidetracked by him. "Come on," he urged. "We'll have a good time dancing. Marty's on Friday night is fun."

"Until the fights break out."

"That doesn't happen often and if it does, we'll get out of there. I have no intention of spending any part of my night in a brawl."

"So it's two-stepping and eating."

He caught her braid in his hand again as he gazed into her eyes. "Plus some kissing."

She drew a deep breath, wanting him to lean closer and kiss her now yet knowing at the same time that she shouldn't want any such thing.

His phone rang and he looked at it. "I have to go, so let's look at the pumps another time. I have an appointment, but I thought as long as I was close, I'd come say hello. Tomorrow night can't come soon enough." He looked at her as if he still had something he wanted to say. Silence settled between them and she wondered what it was and what was keeping him from saying it.

"I've missed being with you," he finally said. He placed his hands on her shoulders, and an odd expression came over his face. "You seem shorter."

She laughed. "I am. I'm not in my high heels like last weekend."

"Oh, yeah," he said, still staring at her. "But you weren't always wearing heels last weekend," he added in a low voice. "Oh, dang," he said, on a ragged exhale. "I shouldn't, but I'm going to anyway." Pulling her closer, he kissed her.

Her heart thudded and she couldn't catch her breath. His kiss was thorough and sexy, making her heart race. And she responded to it instantly.

When he released her, he was breathing hard. "I have to go. I'll see you tomorrow night at six. Leave your hair down so I can see if it looks as good as I think it did last weekend." As she laughed, he grinned while he placed his hands on her waist to pick her up and set her on the other side of the fence. She remembered how easily he'd carried her in his arms Saturday night. He went back to his pickup in long strides, climbed in, waved and drove away.

Her lips still tingled as she stood there staring after him in a daze. "I should have said no," she whispered to herself. "I should not be going out with him. He's still Tony, all alpha male, a man I've always fought with."

Each hour she spent with him only meant more trouble. She knew that as well as she knew her own name. But she'd already accepted, and besides, it was just dinner and dancing, in a place with lots of people. And talking about water. Far from romantic. She wasn't going back to his ranch afterward. Their evening together would be meaningless.

So why couldn't she wait for tomorrow night?

Lindsay studied herself in the mirror while her two Australian shepherd dogs lay nearby on the floor. It was ten to six; Tony would be here any minute. Time for a last check in the mirror. She'd brushed her hair, curled it slightly in long, spiral curls and finally tied it behind her head with a blue silk scarf. She wore a black Resistol, a denim blouse with bling, washed jeans with bling on the hip pockets and her fancy black hand-tooled boots.

She turned to her dogs and each raised his head.

"I promise you, Tony Milan will not be invited inside tonight. When he comes to the door, don't bark at him and don't bite him."

Both animals thumped their tails as she patted their heads and left the room. The dogs followed her to the front room, where she could watch the drive.

In minutes she heard Tony's pickup approach the house. Hurrying to the door, she turned to tell the dogs to sit. As soon as they did, she opened the door. The sight of Tony took her breath away, just as it had when she had seen him yesterday. His black hat, long-sleeved black Western shirt, tight jeans and black boots made him look 100 percent gorgeous cowboy.

She kept a smile on her face as he approached, even as she silently reassured herself there was no way an attraction between them could possibly develop into anything meaningful. With Tony that was impossible and she was certain he felt the same way. As the dogs barked, she gave them commands that caused them to stop, and they came forward quietly to meet Tony, who patted their heads.

"Hi, cowboy," she said.

"Oh, yeah, you don't go out with cowboys. Well, consider this a business dinner," he said, his eyes twinkling.

"Of course. And business kisses."

"Who said one word about kisses?" he asked, his voice lowering a notch as he placed his hand on the jamb over her head. While she looked up at him, her pulse raced.

"I thought there might be a few kisses as well as dinner."

"We could just skip dinner and go inside and you can show me your bedroom."

She smiled and tapped his chest. "What finesse. I think not. You promised dancing and barbecue."

"Whatever the beautiful lady wants," he said, sounding serious, as if he had stopped joking and flirting. She wanted to step into his arms and kiss him. Then she remembered Tony had broken more than a couple of hearts with his "love 'em and leave 'em" ways.

"Let me turn on the alarm, lock up and we can go," she said in a breathless voice that she hoped he wouldn't notice.

"Sure thing." As she moved back, his eyes raked her body. "Each time I see you, you look fantastic."

"Thank you." She said goodbye to the dogs, who now sat near his feet. "You must have a way with dogs. They don't usually take to strangers."

"Women, children and dogs," Tony said.

"I suppose I have to agree on the women and dogs because that's definitely proven. I don't know about children."

"They love me, too," he said with humor in his voice. "Ask your nephew, Scotty."

Smiling, she switched on the alarm and stepped out with him, hearing the lock click.

He linked her arm in his and they walked to his red pickup.

"Allow me," he said as he held the door for her. She climbed in, aware of his constant scrutiny.

"I do love tight jeans," he said, closing the door behind her.

Laughing, she watched him walk around the pickup, feeling excitement mount as she looked forward to being with him again.

"Some of my family has called me to ask about our evening. My guess is that yours has called you," she said, turning toward him as much as her seat belt allowed. She could hardly believe she was sitting here next to him. Her anticipation of this night with him had built all day.

There still was no danger of it becoming a habit for either of them, just one more night—only a few hours of dancing and talking and, maybe, kisses at her door. As they turned on the road toward the county highway, she gripped his arm. "Tony, look over there in the trees. That's a wolf."

Tony followed the direction of her hand and looked toward a stand of scrub oaks. He didn't see any animal. "I don't see anything and there are no wolves in Texas."

"There's one on my ranch. Look."

She was insistent, so he slowed and backed up, stretching his arm over the back of the seat as he reversed the car around the curve. He saw a furry gray animal at the edge of the trees.

"That has to be a coyote," he said. "It looks like a wolf, but it's not. There aren't any in Texas."

"It's too big and furry to be a coyote," she said. As they

watched, the animal turned and disappeared into the darkness of the trees.

"That animal didn't really look like a dog," Tony said, putting the car in gear and continuing to drive. "Well, we've always got wild animals around here. My money's on a coyote."

"It's a gray wolf. They have them now in New Mexico, and a wolf doesn't know state boundaries. They could easily roam into Texas and probably already have. That was only a matter of time. Remember, there's an old legend around these parts about a gray wolf roaming West Texas and anyone who tames him will have one wish granted."

Tony glanced at her with an exaggerated leer. "I know what my wish would be," he said, his gaze sweeping over her.

She laughed. "You lusty man. You've got no chance of taming it. You'd have to catch the wolf first." She returned to her earlier topic. "About our families..."

"Yeah," Tony said. "Wyatt called me Tuesday morning and said we're the hot topic in Verity."

"Imagine that. Me—the hot topic in Verity. Well, let them talk. It'll die down soon because there won't be enough to talk about."

He cast a glance at her. "I'll bet some new guys have asked you out since last Saturday night."

"They have," she said, "but I turned each one down. A couple were at the auction and a couple heard about the auction," she said, having no intention of telling him six guys who saw her Saturday night had asked her out and three who had simply heard about the auction had called and one more had dropped by the ranch.

"All ranchers, I suppose."

"Ranchers, cowboys and an auctioneer from Fort Worth. No way will I get involved with any of them."

"I can understand that, except you're with me tonight."

She smiled. "Maybe you've moved into the classification of an old friend. Besides, there's no danger of involvement for either one of us. I figure this for our last time together."

"You're probably right," he said.

"You can dance, you're fun, and after last weekend, we're civil to each other. I'm sure we'll have a good time."

"I agree about the good time. I can't wait to get you on the dance floor."

"Also, I want something from you."

He shot her a quick glance and then his attention went back to the road. "What can I do for you?" he asked evenly, but his voice had changed, taken on the all-business tone that she was more familiar with.

"I'm trying to see if I can finagle an invitation to your ranch."

He smiled. "Darlin', I thought you'd never ask! I'll take you home with me tonight."

"Cool it, cowboy. I just want to take you up on your earlier offers to look at one of your water pumps."

His smile disappeared and she wondered if he wanted to turn around now and take her home. "Sure, Lindsay. Tell me when you want to come."

His voice had turned solemn and a muscle now worked in his jaw. She knew she was annoying him, but she wanted to see for herself if he still had his old water pumps.

"Thanks, Tony. I appreciate your offer. You told me to come look."

"So I did," he answered, and then he became silent as they drove on the empty road.

After they reached the county road, he glanced at her

once again. "Lindsay, if that's what you wanted tonight, and why you accepted, do you still want to go?"

"But, Tony," she said in a sultry voice, "that wasn't the sole purpose of accepting your offer to go dancing tonight." She ran her fingers lightly along his thigh. "I also remember how much fun and sexy you can be."

She received another one of his glances and saw him inhale deeply. "Then I'm glad you're here, darlin'. That makes the evening much better. 'Fun and sexy,' huh? I'll try to live up to that description."

She laughed. "I'm sure you will," she said.

Flirting with him made the drive seem shorter, and he flirted in return, causing her to forget about water pumps.

When they reached the roadside honky-tonk, loud music greeted them outside the log building. Inside, they found a booth in the dark, crowded room that held a few local people she knew but more that she didn't.

As soon as they had two beers on the table, Tony asked her to dance. The band, made up of a fiddler, drummer and piano player, had couples doing a lively two-step. As they stepped into the group, Tony held her hands, staying close beside her as they circled the room, and then he turned her, so she danced backward as he led. His gaze locked with hers. Desire was evident in the depths of his eyes as he watched her while they danced. She had his full attention and she tingled beneath his gaze and forgot about her problems.

They danced past midnight and after they returned to their table, he leaned closer. "Ready to leave? We can't talk in here anyway."

When she nodded, he stood, waiting as she slid out of the booth to walk out with him. The air was warm outside, the music fading as they climbed into his pickup.

Light from the dash highlighted his prominent cheekbones, but his eyes were in shadow. The ambience reminded her of their night together, when the dim light of his condo bedroom had shielded his eyes from her view. The memories stirred her as she recalled making love with him. She had tried to avoid thinking about him all week, yet here she was with him. This was crazy. She had to get over Tony, forget him and go on with her life. No way did she want to think about their lovemaking or give him a hint that she would ever want to make love to him again.

As they approached her ranch house, lights blazed from it. "Looks like you have a house filled with people."

"I leave it that way. I don't like to come home to a dark, empty house. And I leave some lights for the dogs," she explained. "Drive around to the back door. It'll be easier for me."

He drove through her wrought iron gates, which closed automatically, and did as she instructed. "I can tell you a better way to avoid a dark, empty house. Come home with me." He unbuckled his seat belt and turned to her. "My house will be neither dark nor empty, and I promise you some fun."

She smiled at him, able to see his eyes now; their blue depths seemed to sparkle even in the darkness. "Thanks, but I belong here. Besides, we agreed on the parameters for tonight."

"It's temptation. You're temptation, Lindsay. Beyond my wildest imaginings," he said, leaning forward to unlock her seat belt. As he did, his lips nuzzled her throat while his fingers caressed her nape. Then he turned to get out of the truck and strode around to open her door for her.

He draped his arm across her shoulders as they walked to her door. "Tonight was fun. I could dance with you for hours. There are a lot of things I could do with you for hours."

Her insides tightened and heated, but she forced a grin. "Is playing chess one of them?" she asked, trying to lighten the moment and get his mind off making love.

"No, chess is not what I had in mind at all," he said as he stopped and turned her to face him in the yard under the darkness of a big oak. As he slipped his arm around her waist, her heart thudded. He leaned close to trail kisses on her neck, her ear. "No, what I want to do is hold you close, kiss you until you melt," he said in a deep, husky voice.

His words worked the same magic on her as his lips and hands. Her knees felt weak and she wanted his mouth on hers. Forgetting all her intentions to keep the evening light, she slipped her arm around his neck and raised her mouth for his kiss.

"Why do I find you so damn irresistible?" she asked.

The moment his mouth touched hers, her heart thudded out of control. More than anything she wanted a night with him, wanted to ask him in, but she intended to stick with her promise to herself to say goodbye to him at her door. He deepened the kiss, his tongue stroking hers, slowly and sensually, and she could barely remember what promise she was thinking about. He was aroused, ready to make love, and she, too, ached to take him to her bedroom and have another night like before.

She didn't know how long they had kissed when she finally looked up at him. She had no idea where her next words came from. "I better go in now."

He stared at her, his hot gaze filled with desire that wrapped itself around her and held her in its spell. Stepping out of its heat, she turned to walk onto her porch. Reluctantly he followed.

When they entered the house, the dogs greeted them. She turned them into the fenced yard, closed the door and faced him.

Though he didn't ask for one, she wanted to give him an explanation.

"Tony, we both agreed last weekend was an anomaly. As special as it was, it's over and we need to leave it over. I don't want an affair and I don't think you do, either. With our families intermarried, we would complicate our lives. We're not really all that compatible anyway. I'm too serious for you and you're too much a playboy for me. If I have an affair, I want it long-term, with commitment. You're not the type for that."

"Don't second-guess me, Lindsay. You're incredibly desirable."

"Do you really want us to get deeply involved?"

He inhaled and gazed at her while seconds ticked past.

"I think that's an answer," she said, "and I agree with it."

"There will never be a time when I can look at you and honestly say I don't want you. I—" He stopped when she placed her fingers against his lips.

"Shh. Don't say things that you don't really know."

Kissing her fingers before she took them away, he nodded as he released a breath. "Okay, so we say good-night now. But I'm not going without a goodbye kiss."

He reached out to take off her hat and toss it onto a nearby chair along with his. "Hats get in the way sometimes," he said as he pulled loose the silk scarf that held her hair behind her head and dropped it into her hat. She shook her head and her hair swung across her shoulders to frame her face.

"You're beautiful, Lindsay," he whispered before his mouth covered hers. He kissed her hard, a passionate kiss that tempted her to throw away common sense and invite him upstairs for one more fabulous night.

She felt his arousal, knew he was as ready to make love as she.

But suddenly, before she could speak, he released her. "Good night, Lindsay. If I don't go right now, I won't go at all. I know what you really want is for me to leave." Before she could move, he turned and hurried out the door.

She fled to her bedroom before she called him to come back. Her heart pounded and she ached with longing for him. How could she feel this way about Tony? A Milan, and her nemesis for so many years?

She had to get beyond this heart-pounding reaction she had to him. She couldn't afford to see him again because each time bound her more closely to him.

He had walked out of her life tonight and there wasn't any reason for him to come back into it. At least not in the immediate future. Things would always happen that would cause them to see each other, but her usual encounters with Tony had been only three or four times a year.

When she had asked him if she could come to his ranch and look at one of his pumps, the question had made him angry. Would he be even angrier if she actually went to his ranch? He probably would, but she was going anyway to see for herself whether he had been truthful. It had been ingrained in her by her family not to trust a Milan and she found it difficult to trust Tony on ranch matters.

And personal matters? After last weekend, she might have to answer that question differently.

She lay across the bed, the lights out, and as thoughts of Tony swirled in her mind, she knew she'd never sleep tonight. Not when she was wishing she were with him, in his arms, naked beside him. Would he sleep? Knowing him, she figured he'd sleep like a bear in winter.

She closed her eyes against the tears that stung them. Tony was out of her life—where he should be. There was no way they had any future as a couple. She'd accomplished all she'd set out to do that night at the bachelor auction. She'd bid on him to butter him up, to make him more amenable. At least that seemed to have worked. With any luck, the fights had stopped or at least changed to simple quarrels. If that had happened, it all would have been worthwhile.

There'd be no more calls from Tony after tonight. The thought swept her with a sense of loss. She shook her head as if she could shake away the feeling. How long would it take her life to get back to normal?

Five

He hadn't been ready to tell her goodbye tonight. The whole time he'd cruised down the driveway he'd watched her house in the rearview mirror, fighting the urge to turn around.

If he let himself, Tony could envision the scene clearly. He'd stop sharply, his tires spewing dirt and gravel as he spun around and gunned his engine. When he pulled up at her back porch, she'd be there throwing open the door, and she'd run to him just as he stepped out of the truck. He'd pick her up in his arms and carry her back into her house, right up to her bedroom. They wouldn't say a word to each other; they wouldn't need to. They'd simply make love. And it would be amazing.

A nice image, he had to admit. But one that wouldn't happen.

Instead, he drove the pickup onto the county road toward his own ranch.

He couldn't help but feel tense, and not just sexually.

He'd been looking forward to this night with Lindsay, and to say it hadn't ended the way he'd hoped would be an understatement. But she was right. They had no future. And Lindsay wasn't the type of woman to have an affair without a future.

And she was too serious, just as she said.

Not to mention the whole business with her wanting to see his water pumps. Damn, she still didn't believe that he hadn't installed bigger pumps to steal her water. She wanted to see it with her own two eyes. Because he was a Milan, no doubt, and Milans never told the truth!

He banged the palm of his hand on the steering wheel. He needed to forget her.

As he drove along the darkened road, he turned on the radio, but the guy who sang—some guy who'd won one of those ubiquitous TV reality shows—strummed a soulful guitar and sang about the cute filly he was pining for. Tony didn't want to hear it. He shut it off. He had enough of his own problems with his own cute filly. A spirited one, at that.

He had to let out a laugh at the thought of Lindsay knowing he had referred to her as a filly. She'd probably take out her shotgun and fill him with buckshot.

The drive home seemed endless, but by the time he pulled onto the long driveway up to his ranch house, he knew what he had to do. He had to forget everything about Lindsay Calhoun, starting with last Saturday night. From the moment he'd seen her in that red dress all the way to tonight. As sexy, as enticing, as appealing as Lindsay was, she wasn't the woman for him. They could never be together. She was commitment with a capital C, and that was one thing he couldn't—wouldn't—ever be willing to give.

He entered the house and went up to bed, not even bothering to turn on a light.

* * *

She hadn't bothered to turn on the light.

For some reason, that thought struck her as she woke up. She remembered running up to her room, in the dark, after Tony left, and throwing herself on the bed, sad and uncharacteristically near tears. She thought she'd never sleep tonight, but apparently she had.

She felt beside her and at her feet, but the dogs weren't in their usual position. Then she remembered. She'd let them out when she got home and then forgotten about them. They'd probably gone over to the bunkhouse for the night.

She sat up, glancing at the clock on her bedside table to see it was after three in the morning. A long, sad howl sent chills down her spine and she ran to the window to look out. Another sad howl filled the night.

Moonlight splashed over open spaces and something moved. Chills ran down her spine again as she saw the wolf standing at the edge of a grove of trees. As she watched, it threw back its head and howled again.

She shivered. For the first time since being on the ranch, she felt alone and didn't like it. She wished she had kept the dogs with her and hoped no one at the bunkhouse turned them out, because she didn't want them tangling with a wolf. She also hoped no one at the bunkhouse got his gun. The men were good shots. If they wanted to kill the wolf, they would surely succeed. She grabbed her phone to call her foreman, thought about it and decided it would be ridiculous to wake him. When morning came, she would talk to Abe about the four-legged intruder.

Another lonely howl caused a fresh batch of shivers to crawl up her spine. Impulsively, telling herself she shouldn't, she called the one person she thought of.

She felt silly when Tony answered, and she suddenly

wished she hadn't called him. But she'd awakened him and she had to explain why.

"Sorry, Tony. I know I woke you."

"Lindsay? Are you okay?" he asked, in a surprisingly clear, alert voice.

"I'm fine, Tony." Now that she had him on the phone she couldn't seem to tell him about the wolf. What did she expect him to do about it?

"Okay then, darlin', what's on your mind at…3:17 a.m.?"

"I feel really silly now."

"Lindsay, you didn't call me in the middle of the night to tell me you feel silly."

"The wolf/coyote/dog—except it looks like a wolf— is howling near my bedroom. I can see it and the animal sounds hurt."

"All animals sound hurt when they howl. So? I know you're a crack shot even with that big .45 you own. Take him out and go back to sleep."

"A gunshot would wake everyone on the ranch and create an uproar. Anyway, I can't kill him. Or her. He or she sounds pitiful and eerie, and for the first time since I've owned the ranch I don't like being here alone."

"I'm coming over."

"No, Tony. I just wanted to hear your voice. Don't get up and come over."

"I can be there in a few minutes."

"Stay in bed," she said, hearing another long howl and looking at the animal standing half in the moonlight and half in shadow. "I feel sorry for it. It sounds hurt and lonesome."

"I'll be over in a flash. I can really take your mind off the wolf, howls or no howls."

She smiled and sat back in the chair by the window.

"You're succeeding right now and you just stay home. We'll both be better off."

She didn't want a repeat of the scene they'd endured only hours ago at her back door. Watching him walk away was hard enough then; she couldn't go through seeing him—and losing him—again.

"That may be true for you, but if I come over, I would definitely be better off."

Despite herself, she laughed softly. "You make me feel so much better. But I still think you should stay home."

"Lindsay, I'm already pulling on my jeans."

"Don't. I really mean it. I feel better now and I can go back to sleep, and I know you can roll over and go to sleep the minute your head is on the pillow." She refused to picture him taking off his jeans and getting back into bed, shirtless and sexy.

"Fine," he said. "The guys will take care of the animal for you and, hereafter, you won't have to listen to it howl again."

"I don't know why, but I feel sorry for it. Unless it kills some of the livestock, I'd hate for them to shoot it."

"Well, this is a change. You're usually pretty damn tough and I know you've shot plenty of wildlife."

"Now how would you know that?"

"The guys talk. And I remember a few marksmanship competitions over the years. Come to think of it, you haven't participated in any in a long time."

"Nope. It doesn't seem to matter any longer. When I first got the ranch, I felt I had to prove that I could handle running the place and a few other things. I don't feel that way any longer."

"I would think not. Half the ranchers around here call you about their animals."

"Not really half, but a few have," she said. She settled

back in the chair to talk, forgetting about everything but the sound of his voice, soothing and smooth as it settled around her in the darkness. It was an hour later when they finally said goodbye and she went to bed. That's when she realized the howls had stopped long ago, but she hadn't actually noticed when, thanks to Tony.

As the next week passed, Lindsay tried to keep busy and struggled to stop thinking about Tony, but that was impossible. She heard nothing from him for eight more days, but, instead of forgetting about him—something she once could easily do—she thought about him constantly, to the point where she had been distracted at work.

It was Thursday, in the middle of a hot, dry afternoon, after she'd helped move steers to another pasture, when her phone rang and she saw it was Tony. She pulled her truck off the road into the shade of an oak and opened the windows.

"It's Tony. I thought it was time to see if you want to come look at the pumps on my water wells."

She was surprised, to say the least. Even though he'd offered, she'd never really expected him to have her over to his ranch—because she still figured he had installed new and bigger pumps. She glanced at her watch. "Give me about two hours and I'll be there. Tell everyone I'm coming so they don't send me away if they see me."

"Nobody's going to send you away and my foreman knows I was going to call you. Come on over. See you in two hours," he said, and ended the connection.

She looked at her phone for seconds, as if she could see Tony. Was he up to some trickery to convince her that he still had his old pumps and had just dug deeper?

She would never tell Tony, but she had already started checking into having her wells dug deeper, and Tony had been right. If she went deeper, there was still water

in the aquifer, and when the rains finally came, that de-
pleted water would be replenished and everything would
be like it was.

She had already told the men she was headed home,
so she started her truck and drove back to her house
to shower. She changed into washed jeans, boots and a
short-sleeved blue cotton shirt. She knew Tony liked her
hair down and not fastened, but she was back at home and
she didn't care to change her appearance, so she braided
her hair and got her wide-brimmed black hat.

She hadn't been to Tony's ranch house even though she
had seen pictures of it on the web, along with a map of his
ranch land. As she approached, she looked at the sprawling two-story ranch house that appeared even larger than
hers. A porch ran across the front and a wide circle drive
joined a walk leading to the front porch.

Flower beds surrounded the house with rock and cac-
tus gardens, plants well adapted to the drought that usually hit West Texas. As she approached, Tony crossed his
porch, coming to meet her, his long legs covering the distance. His hair was combed and he had on a clean short-
sleeved blue-and-red-plaid shirt, tucked into his jeans.
She smiled, happy to see him again.

Tony opened the door of her truck and watched her
step out.

"Oh, lady, you do look great," he said, his gaze sweeping over her and making her tingle and momentarily forget why she was here.

"And hello to you. Thank you."

"You've never been to my home, have you?"

"Nope, I haven't. And you haven't been in mine, yet.
Not really," she amended, as she thought about last week
and how he'd barely made it through her back door before he left.

"Well, I hope to remedy that soon," he said.

"We'll see."

They stepped into an entry foyer that held a full-length mahogany mirror, two hat racks, hooks for coats, shelves that housed several pairs of boots. Stepping through the hallway, they came to a huge kitchen with state-of-the-art-equipment and luxurious dark wood cabinetry. The adjoining family room held a stone fireplace, a big-screen television, a game table, as well as a desk with two computers and other electronic devices.

"All the comforts of home, huh?" she asked. "It's a marvelous home."

"I suspect you have one to match," he remarked.

"Odd that we've never been in each other's houses in all the years we've known each other," she said.

"There's a lot we didn't do in all the years we've known each other," he said, setting her nerves on edge. "C'mon, I'll show you more."

They walked down a wide hall with Western paintings and beautiful tapestries that surprised her. The hall held finely crafted furniture, double front doors where floor-to-ceiling windows let in light and offered a grand view of the front of his property.

"Very beautiful, Tony. And a little surprising."

"You probably pictured me in a log cabin with brass spittoons and bawdy paintings," he said grinning.

She smiled. "Not that extreme, just maybe a little more rustic than this. After all, you're a rancher at heart. This fancy home could belong to a Chicago stockbroker."

He shrugged. "It's comfortable, what I like and a haven when I come home."

"That I understand." She followed him as he directed her down another hallway.

"I don't really know much about you as a person," she

said when he stopped outside a closed door. "Just as an annoyance in my life—until this month," she said.

"I'm glad you added that last part. Here, Lindsay," he said, ushering her into a suite with a sitting room that held floor-to-ceiling windows affording a panoramic view of a terrace and fields beyond it where horses grazed. "Here's my living room. Want to see my bedroom next?"

Smiling at him, she shook her head. "I think we're skirting the edge of temptation too much as it is. Thanks, I'll pass."

"Okay, then, on to the study."

They went down the hall to another room, as elegant as the last, with leather furniture, oils on the walls, heavy shelves and polished cherrywood floors.

As she looked around, he said, "We can finish the tour later." He glanced out the window. "Because I want you to see one of the pumps before the sun goes down."

"Good idea," she said. She wanted to see it in daylight, too, because if it really was his old pump, it would have rust.

"I'm ready."

He placed a hand on the small of her back. "So am I," he said in the husky tone he'd had when making love.

She stepped back. "You're not helping the situation. We agreed that we were not pursuing..." She searched but couldn't find the word she wanted. "Not pursuing this," she said, "any further." She tried to sound forceful, but her words sounded hollow, even to herself.

Tony must have thought so, too, because he said nothing. He merely stepped close and placed his hands on her waist. Her breathing became shallow and erratic as his steady gaze met her eyes and then lowered to her mouth.

Dimly the thought nagged at her that it had been a

mistake to come here, but she wanted to see if he had been truthful with her.

She couldn't step away or protest. She saw the desire in the blue-green depths of his eyes and her mouth went dry. She wanted his kiss just one more time.

He leaned down to kiss her, a hot, possessive kiss that made her feel he wanted her with all his being. Her heart pounded as she wrapped her arms around his neck and kissed him back, once again trying to make him remember this moment and be as conflicted as she was.

Her world spun away, lost in Tony's kisses that set her ablaze. She felt his hands drifting up her back, then moving forward to lightly caress her breasts.

"Tony," she whispered, unable to tell him to stop, yet knowing they should.

She caught his wrists and leaned back. "This isn't why I came," she whispered, and then stepped away. "Water well pump, remember?" she asked, unable to get any firmness in her voice.

"When you're ready, we'll go," he said. He stood so close that her heart pounded and it took all the willpower she had to move away.

"We both have to do better than this tonight."

"I intend to do a lot better," he said, teasing and leering at her, causing her to laugh.

"You're hopeless and headed for trouble, and you're taking me with you." She smoothed down her shirt and stood tall. "I'm ready to look at that pump now."

"One thing—in case you think I might have one old pump for moments like this and the rest are new, I'll let you select which one we go see," he said. She went with him to his desk, a massive cherry table. He opened a drawer and pulled out a map, which he unfolded. "This is a map of the ranch with the water wells circled in yellow. You can select one. If you want to look at all of them, we can."

She gave him a searching look. "I'm beginning to believe you and feel really foolish."

"This is why you came. Pick the wells, Lindsay," he instructed.

She looked again and pointed to one the shortest distance from the house.

"Is that all? I want you totally satisfied when you go home." He said the last words in the tone of voice he used when he was flirting with her. He was back to sexy innuendos, which kept her thinking about his kisses and lovemaking.

"Tony, you've got to stop that," she said, unable to suppress another laugh. He grinned and took her arm.

"I don't think you really want me to. You say those words, but your body, your eyes, your voice are giving you away, darlin'."

"Time to go, Tony," she said, trying to resist him, the sensible thing to do.

They drove to the well and she could see the rust on the pump from yards away. She turned to place her hand on his arm. "Tony, I'm sorry. I've misjudged you and accused you of things you didn't do."

He turned to face her. "You don't want to see another well?"

She shook her head, "No. I apologize."

"Apology accepted."

"I've already taken your advice and called to see about digging my wells deeper."

"Good. C'mon, let's go home and have some juicy steaks."

She knew she should say no, but she couldn't. She

had been wrong about him—he had been telling her the truth all along.

She thought of all the times she had been told not to trust a Milan. Her grandmother had practically drummed it into her head. But her brother had married Tony's sister and trusted her fully. Shouldn't she have learned anything from Jake?

They rode back in silence, but when they stepped into his kitchen, she had to apologize again. She felt that bad.

"Tony, again, I'm so sorry. I—"

He turned to her and put his hands on her waist. "Don't worry about it, it doesn't matter now. This is all that matters."

He tilted her chin up, and she saw the flicker in his eyes and knew when the moment changed. He drew her into his embrace and kissed her, holding her tightly and kissing her thoroughly until she was breathless. With a moan of pleasure, she slipped her arm around his neck and another around his waist to hold him tightly, wanting his kiss in spite of all her intentions of resisting him.

When he released her, he smiled. "That's better," he said. "Let's have a drink and I'll start the steaks."

Though she knew she should go home for a quiet dinner alone, she nodded instead. She tingled from his kiss and wanted more. Each kiss was a threat to her heart and she promised herself she would stop seeing him after this evening. It was just one more night.

She drew a deep breath as her throat went dry. "We weren't going to do this."

"So we're together three times instead of two. Seeing each other will end and we both know it, so what does tonight hurt?" he asked.

"You make it sound like something silly for me to protest."

"You know I want you to stay. It won't be a big deal, Lindsay."

With her heart drumming, she watched him walk to a bar. Who would have thought it? A cowboy who could turn her world upside down, who had become the sexiest, most handsome man she had ever known. How could Tony have become important to her, able to set her heart pounding just by walking into a room where she was?

What seemed worse, the more she knew him, the better she liked him and the more she thought of him. That realization scared her. She didn't want to respect him, admire him and like him. He was still Tony, who had to run everything all the time. Physically, she was intensely attracted to him, but it was beginning to spill over into other aspects of their lives and that scared her.

Never in her life had she been attracted to someone who could put her way of life at risk—until now.

To protect her own lifestyle, she had to make tonight the last time she would socialize with him. She had to break off seeing him before her life was in shambles and her heart broken.

Could she adhere to that…or was it too late?

Six

He wasn't in the kitchen when she came back from freshening up in the powder room. Where had he gone?

She saw a column of gray smoke spiraling skyward and followed it to the glassed-in sitting room where she saw him outside at a grill. When she went out, he turned to smile at her. Tall, lean and strong, he kept her heart racing. His blue-eyed gaze drifted over her and she could see his approval.

"The steak smells wonderful," she said.

"Thanks. We have tossed salad and twice-baked potatoes, too."

"When did you fix all that? Twice-baked potatoes? You planned this?"

"No. I have Gwynne, a cook who has gone home now. She fixes dinners and leaves them for me. The potatoes were frozen and easy to thaw and heat. She lives in her own place here on the ranch and cooks five days a week."

"And what do you do the other two days?"

"Eat alone," he said.

"I can imagine," she remarked, thinking of women she knew he had taken out.

He chuckled as he turned to look at the steaks.

The terrace was broad, running across the back of the house and along the bright blue swimming pool that looked so inviting.

"What do you want to drink? Iced tea, wine, cold beer, martini—you name what you'd like."

"With a drive home tonight, I think iced tea is a good choice."

"I'll get you that, but I'd be happy to drive you home tonight."

"I'll take the tea," she answered, smiling at him, wanting to accept his offer, wanting to stay all night, but determined to do what she should.

In minutes he brought her a tall glass of tea and he held a cold beer. "Shall we sit where I can keep an eye on the steaks?"

All the time they talked, she was aware of him sitting close. His hand rested on her shoulder, rubbing it lightly, or on her nape, his warm fingers drifting in feathery caresses, all small touches that were heightening desire. Was it going to be easy to forget the times spent with him? Was she going to miss him or think about him when they parted for good? She knew the answers to both questions. What she was uncertain about was whether she could resist him.

Soon they sat down to eat in his cool, informal dining area.

"Once again, I'm surprised and impressed. You're quite a cook, Tony. The steaks are delicious."

"Thank you. Our own beef and my own cooking. Ta-da."

When she laughed, he shook his head.

"I need to make an improvement," he said, reaching out to unfasten one more button of her shirt and push it open to reveal her lush curves. His warm fingers brushed her lightly and she drew a sharp breath, longing for his touch.

She hoped what she wanted didn't show. She could barely eat. All she wanted was to be in his arms. In some part of her mind she wondered if he had an ulterior motive for inviting her to see the pumps.

He turned on the charm during dinner, smiling and telling her stories about his family and funny incidents when he started as a rancher. They sat for hours after they finished their steaks, laughing and talking over coffee, until she realized the sun had gone down a long time ago. She stood. "It's getting late, Tony. I should go home." She picked up her plate. Instantly Tony took her dish from her hands.

"None of that. Gwynne will be here in the morning and will take care of it."

"So then I should be going," she said, trying to stick to what she felt she should do.

Placing his hands on her shoulders, making her tingle in anticipation, he turned her to face him.

"Don't go home tonight, Lindsay. You have choices—you can sleep downstairs alone or upstairs with me, but stay. I don't want you to drive back tonight."

"Tony," she said, her heart drumming as she looked into his blue-green eyes, "you know I should go. We've talked about this."

He stepped closer to wrap his arms around her and kiss her. When she knew she was on the verge of agreeing to stay, she stepped out of his embrace.

"I have to go home," she said breathlessly.

He nodded and watched as she straightened her blouse and turned for the door.

Draping his arm across her shoulders, he walked her to her pickup.

"I know you're doing what's sensible. We have different lifestyles. Even so, I don't want you to go."

"I have to," she said and turned to climb into her pickup. She smiled at him. "Thanks for dinner and for showing me your water pump."

"Sure. I'll call you," he said, and closed the pickup door.

He stood on the driveway watching her as she drove away. She glanced several times at the rearview mirror and he still stood watching. Then she rounded a curve and he was gone from view.

She trembled with longing, wanting to stay, telling herself over and over that she was doing the right thing and the smart thing. She had no future with Tony. Far from it, he would be a threat to her and her ranch. Why didn't that knowledge make her feel better?

She tried to stop thinking about his kisses, the laughs they had shared. What she was doing was for the best. She missed him, but she was not brokenhearted after an affair that Tony had ended, something she wanted to avoid with all her being.

The auction had been worth the money if she got friendliness and cooperation from him. She knew he would never stop telling her what she should do, but they could have a more neighborly relationship. In a week she would probably feel differently about him if she stopped seeing him and talking to him.

Tony stood a few minutes after Lindsay drove out of sight. Longing for her tore at him and was impossible for him to ignore.

How could he have so much fun with her now, find her

so desirable when not long ago they were at each other's throats over every issue?

He knew the answer to his question. She was the sexiest, best-looking, most fun woman he had ever known. The realization still shook him.

Feeling empty, he stared at the road, wishing she would turn around and come back. Back into his arms and into his bed tonight.

He shouldn't miss her—he had never missed a woman this much or given one this much thought when he wasn't with her.

Of all the women in Texas, why did it have to be Lindsay who had turned his life topsy-turvy?

With a long sigh, he turned to go inside, knowing he wouldn't be able to stop thinking about her or sleep peacefully tonight.

As he walked back to his house, he saw a light in one of the barns. On impulse, to avoid being alone, he changed direction and strolled to the barn, where he found Keane nailing up more shelves in the tack room.

"I wondered who was working. Need help?"

"Yep. In a minute. I need a break. If you have time, four hands will be better than two trying to get these shelves in place," Keane said as he sat on a crate.

Tony sat on a bale of hay and stretched out his legs. "Lindsay just left and she's happy about my water pumps. She is going to look into doing the same, as we have to get water."

"She can be a nice lady. Good for neighbors to get along."

"It should be more peaceful. I hope it lasts, because she still can be her stubborn self."

"She's not so bad, but you know that now. The people who work for her like her."

"For a time it will probably be better between us."

"I'd bet money on that one," Keane remarked drily. "She's a strong woman who knows what she wants."

"Amen to that. Actually, I don't think we'll see any more of each other in the future."

"Maybe so. You'll work it out, I'm sure."

Tony focused on his foreman because it sounded as if Keane was trying to hold back laughter. "Ready to get back to work?" Tony asked, standing because he wanted to end the conversation about his private life.

"Sure. You can hold one of these boards in place for me."

Silently, Tony followed directions from Keane, but his thoughts drifted to Lindsay. He didn't want to go back to his empty house. He missed her and didn't want to think about her staying or having her in his arms in his bed tonight.

Once Keane stopped to look at him.

"What?"

"You're getting ready to hammer that board in and it's in the wrong place."

Startled, Tony looked at the narrow board he held in his hands. "Sorry," he said, adjusting it as he felt his face heat. He had been lost in thoughts about Lindsay. He made an effort to stop thinking about her and focus on the job at hand.

Tony managed to keep his thoughts on the task and, in minutes, Keane stepped back to look at his completed shelves.

"With your help, we're through," Keane said. "Thanks, boss. That went quickly. I'll put away the tools."

"I'll help," Tony stated, acting quickly. In minutes they parted, Keane for his house and Tony walking back to his, which was dark and empty.

He stepped inside, locked the door and went to the kitchen to get a beer. He carried it out to the patio to sit and gaze at the pool, gardens and fountain while he thought about Lindsay.

He had to get her out of his thoughts. They had no future together and neither one wanted a future together. It still amazed him how much she was in his thoughts.

"Goodbye, Lindsay," he said aloud, as if he could get her out of his thoughts that way. He didn't expect to see her again soon. He tried to ignore the pang that caused.

Lindsay stood in front of the calendar the next morning counting the days. Once and again. No matter how many times she counted it, the results were the same. She had missed her period by almost a couple of weeks now, and that had never happened before. Common sense said there could be a host of reasons and she should give it more time. But could she be pregnant? Tony had taken precautions, but there was always a chance. She knew the statistics.

Anxiety washed over her with the force of a tidal wave, and she pulled out her desk chair to sit down.

After a few minutes, she reminded herself that women were late all the time without it meaning they were pregnant and she should give it a few more days. No sense worrying needlessly. She simply put it out of her mind and got ready for work.

But when the next two days passed with no change, she had to get a home pregnancy test. She couldn't get it in Verity or any town in the surrounding counties where she knew nearly everyone.

She was having Tony's baby. She knew it. Shock buffeted her. How could she deal with it?

She was going to have to figure out how to deal with

it. She picked up her phone to send a text to her foreman. Something's come up. I'll call later.

In a minute she received a reply: Okay. She put her head in her hands. If only she could undo everything and go back to the way she and Tony had been before the auction. She didn't want to be pregnant with Tony's baby. She'd always thought someday she would marry and have a family. Now she was going to have the family without the marriage.

She didn't want Tony to know yet. She had to have plans in place so he couldn't take over.

She ran her hands through her hair. She wasn't ready for this. Tony would want to be part of his child's life, and he would take charge and tell her what to do the moment he learned she was carrying his baby.

Telling her how to run her ranch would be nothing compared to telling her how to raise a baby.

Their baby.

A Milan baby.

A Milan baby fathered by a man she could never marry.

But their families would want them to marry. Hers would pressure her, just as his would pressure him. She knew he was the family type who would think they should marry for this baby's sake. She would have a bigger fight with Tony than she had ever had before. Running two big ranches and raising a baby together. They wouldn't have a battle—they'd have a war! She put her head in her hands to cry, something she rarely did. How would she cope with this? For once in her life she felt overwhelmed.

For a few minutes as she cried, she let go, swamped by a looming disaster. She raised her head and her gaze fell on a picture of her nephew she had taken when Scotty was two. He was laughing, sitting astride a big horse and

holding the reins. She loved the picture and she loved
Scotty with all her heart and had always hoped she would
have a little boy just like him.

She sat up, dried her eyes and stared at Scotty's picture, pulling it close. She was going to have a baby and
maybe her child would be as wonderful as Scotty. And her
family would stand by her. She had no doubts about that.

She had always avoided dating ranchers until Tony.
When she bought a night with him at the auction, she had
not expected to fall into bed with him or to even want
to see him again.

She should have stuck to her rule of not dating a rancher,
no matter the circumstances. But it had never once occurred to her that she could be attracted to Tony, not until
she had seen him in that tux, looking so sexy, those eyes
that could convey enough desire to melt her.

Logic said to make a doctor's appointment and have
her pregnancy verified by a lab and a professional. She
could get a home kit, but she wanted a doctor's results
to be certain. That was step one. Telling Tony would be
step two and the one that she could not cope with thinking about now.

Why had she ever bid for him in the damn auction?
No undoing that night now, but it was coming back to
haunt her. She needed to plan and to find a good doctor. She couldn't go to a doctor in Verity or anywhere
around the area. Texas might not even be big enough. She
didn't want word getting to Tony until she was ready to
tell him herself. She should fly to a big city, like Tulsa
or Albuquerque, but she didn't know any doctors there.
She thought about Savannah, Mike's pregnant wife who
was from Arkansas.

If Savannah gave her an Arkansas doctor's name, she

could drive to Dallas and then fly to Arkansas without anyone else in the family knowing where she had gone or why. As she thought about her older brother, Mike, she wanted to talk to him and to Savannah. Because of Scotty, she had gotten where she felt close to Mike, and now that he had married Savannah, they would be the ones to talk to about her situation. Savannah had never intended to become pregnant and when her ex-fiancé in Arkansas found out, he had been hateful and hadn't wanted his baby. Lindsay sighed. At least she would never have to worry about that with Tony. It would be just the opposite with Tony. He would want this baby in his life all the time.

Madison, Jake's wife, was expecting, too. That would help soften Jake's attitude about her situation. And Jake liked Tony. Her brothers liked him and their wives did, too. She had been the sole member of her generation to fight him. In fact, it was the older generations of Calhouns that didn't like the Milans. She had heard Destiny talk about her grandmother's intense dislike of Milans. Maybe that had eased up now that Wyatt and Destiny were married, as well as Jake and Madison.

She had always been close to all her brothers, particularly Josh when they were young, so Josh and Abby would give her support. Abby had a heart of gold and would be as kind as Josh.

Looking again at the calendar, she picked up her phone and called Savannah and in minutes made arrangements to see her.

By noon she was showered and dressed. She studied herself in the mirror, turning first one way and then another, knowing it was ridiculous to expect to see any change yet. Her cell phone rang. When she saw it was Tony, she ignored the call.

* * *

Smiling, Savannah opened the back door. "Come in. Mike is out on the ranch somewhere and you said not to call him, so I didn't. Scotty is napping."

"I'll make this short, Savannah. I wanted to talk to just you. Not Mike. And not Scotty right now."

"Sure. Come in," Savannah said, stepping back out of the way and shaking her blond hair away from her face. "Want a cool drink?" Savannah asked.

"Ice water would be fine, and you sit and let me get it and whatever you want to drink. I know this kitchen almost as well as my own."

"I'm a little clumsy, but I'm not feeble. I can get us glasses of water," Savannah said as she turned to wash her hands and get down glasses. Lindsay's gaze ran over Savannah's navy T-shirt and jeans. She knew Savannah's baby was due in October, which was only weeks away now that it was already the first day of September. Savannah's round belly didn't look big enough to deliver in another month. "You don't look very pregnant."

"I feel very, very pregnant. And believe me, there's no such thing as not very pregnant."

Lindsay laughed politely, but she still couldn't cope with the prospect of being pregnant or joke about it. Each time she thought about it, she also wondered how she would ever tell Tony. She had no answer to that one.

In minutes they had glasses of water and sat in the family room. Savannah gazed at her. "I heard you and Tony got along fine on your auction date. And you've been out with him since."

"I suppose it's impossible to keep our going out together private as long as we go out in Texas."

"I don't imagine you can. Both of you know many

people," Savannah said. She sipped her water. "Are you okay, Lindsay?" she asked finally.

"I don't know. That's why I think you're the one to talk to. I do need to keep this secret awhile and I thought about you being from Little Rock. I need to see an obstetrician without my family or anyone else around here knowing except you and Mike. Savannah, I think I'm pregnant with Tony's baby."

"Oh, my word," Savannah said, her blue eyes growing wide. "I know that's a shock."

"It is a shock that I haven't adjusted to, but I want it officially confirmed."

"Maybe you're worrying needlessly."

"I don't think so. I feel it to my bones."

"Oh, my. It'll be better than what I went through, although it led me to Mike. With Tony, it'll be good. He'll marry you, Lindsay. It's obvious you have made peace with each other. And the whole Calhoun family loves Tony. And he's so good to Scotty. Scotty is crazy about Tony even though they don't see each other often."

"I can't imagine Tony wanting to marry me and I don't want to marry Tony. I don't want to marry any rancher. Until Tony, I've never even dated one. Marriage to one would be a perpetual clash because I want to run my ranch my own way and I don't want some other rancher telling me to change the way I do things. And Tony is a take-charge person."

"Oh, dear." Savannah frowned. "You might have a problem."

"I have a big problem."

"Are you sure you're pregnant?"

"About ninety-nine percent, but that's why I want your doctor's name. I should see a doctor before I get Tony all stirred up. Other than you and Mike, I don't want anyone else to know I even suspect I'm pregnant until I verify it. Then I can tell Tony. I haven't even tried a home pregnancy test yet because I'll have to drive so far to get away from everyone I know, but I'm going today." She shook her head. "Even though I know what the outcome will be."

"Let me call my doctor's office and introduce you, then you can get on and make an appointment. Until you have a home test and the lab tests and have a doctor confirm your condition, you don't know for sure. You may not even be pregnant and may be worrying for nothing."

"Hopefully not, but if I had to bet, I'd bet the ranch that I am."

Savannah's eyes widened. "You mean that?"

Lindsay shrugged. "You get a feeling for things, you know?"

"Mike says you have a knack for knowing things and a touch that's just right. He's impressed by your abilities."

"That's nice. He hasn't mentioned that to me."

Savannah laughed. "You're his little sister. He probably doesn't realize he hasn't told you." She stood up. "Let me make that call before Scotty is up or Mike comes home. This doctor is so good about working people into his schedule."

Within the next thirty minutes Lindsay had an appointment in Little Rock on Thursday.

She sat again to face Savannah. "I really thank you for this. That was very nice."

"I'm glad to help. I only hope Mike doesn't suspect anything."

"Savannah, I don't want you to have to keep secrets from Mike. Just make it clear that you two are the only ones I'm telling at this point."

"I can wait a bit to tell Mike. He'll understand."

"You really don't need to, but thanks. I better go."

They walked to the door. "Take care of yourself," Savannah said. "Call me after you see the doctor. I'm your sister-in-law, and I'm also your friend. I can give you my doctor's name in Dallas, too." They gazed at each other and Savannah reached out to hug Lindsay.

"Thanks, Savannah. You're really good for Mike and good for our family."

"He and Scotty and the Calhouns are wonderful for me, too. Take care of yourself."

"I will," Lindsay said, and hurried to her pickup to drive home.

Thursday she drove to Dallas and flew to Little Rock to go to the doctor's office. She was thankful no one would know or question what she was doing or where she was going. The only person who came close was Abe, who had worked for her family since he was seventeen. She saw the questions in his eyes, but he didn't voice them.

The only thing that indicated his feelings was when she told him goodbye.

"Lindsay, if you want me to do anything, let me know," he said, looking intently at her, and she was certain he knew she had something she was hiding.

"Thanks. I will. I'm all right," she answered, looking into his light brown eyes. "I have my phone and if I need anything, I'll call. I'll be back tomorrow about noon."

"Sure," he said. He settled his brown hat on his head, nodded and headed back to the barn as she climbed into her pickup to drive to Dallas.

Now as she got out of the cab in front of the obstetrician's office, she felt her heart start to pound and her palms sweat.

But that anxiety was nothing to what she felt when she came out.

She felt so stressed she had to stop on the sidewalk. She stood staring and not seeing anything in front of her. Hot September sunshine blazed overhead, but chills skidded up her spine. She had known for the past two weeks that she was pregnant, but to have it confirmed by a home pregnancy test and now, to hear it officially announced by a physician after a lab test made it real.

How was she ever going to tell Tony?

Seven

Tony threw himself into work, coming home nights to an empty house that he had never felt alone in before. Constantly, he remembered Lindsay in his arms, and he wanted to talk to her or see her again. Every time he reached for the phone, he stopped, reminding himself she wanted them to break off seeing each other and he should, too, because it was inevitable.

In spite of logic, he missed seeing her. He knew from one of the men who worked for him that she had gone to Dallas and he wondered why and what she was doing there. He would get over her soon because he knew as well as she did, in spite of their truce, they were still the same people and she remained stubborn as ever. It was just a matter of time before there was another conflict between them, something she seemed to thrive on. Though common sense told him that he was better off without her, he missed her in a way he wouldn't have thought possible.

He woke up on Friday morning and she was still on his mind. He knew time would take care of this longing for her, but right now memories of her wouldn't stop coming.

He rose and got ready for a first-thing-in-the-morning meeting with Keane, who had problems with one of their trucks.

Tony stood on his porch with his foreman, who had his hat pushed far enough back on his head to reveal a pale strip on his forehead where his hat always shaded him. His tangled, curly brown hair framed his face. He was shorter than Tony, slightly stocky and the most capable ranch hand Tony had ever had.

"Keane, I heard an animal howling last night. I've seen it before on Lindsay's ranch," he said, remembering the eerie howls that had been so forlorn and sounded like an injured animal. As he had listened, he understood why the howls had unnerved Lindsay and caused her to call. They'd been jarring in the night, even to him. He'd finally got up and retrieved a rifle, switching off yard lights and stepping out on his dark porch. He'd seen it plainly in the moonlight, but he'd paused as he lifted his rifle, remembering Lindsay's request that the animal not be put down. He'd lowered his rifle and walked back inside to lock up, put away his rifle and go back to bed.

"It might be a dog," he told Keane now. "Might be a coyote. Lindsay thinks it's a wolf and she doesn't want it put down unless it starts killing livestock. Pass the word to leave it alone unless it kills something and until we know it isn't a big dog."

"Sure. Have you seen it?"

"Yes. It's big, has black and gray shaggy fur and, frankly, it does resemble a wolf, but I can't imagine it is."

Keane had a faint smile. "You know that old legend."

"If I thought that were possible, which I don't, I'd try to catch and tame the critter and I'd wish for rain."

"Amen to that one," Keane said, glancing at the sky. "Still none in the forecast. No break in the heat, either—over a hundred today. When it does rain, the ground will soak up water like a sponge. It'll just disappear. We need a month of rains."

"Right. Well, I'll see about replacing that truck," Tony said, and turned to go.

While Tony worked all day alongside the men, keeping his hands busy, he couldn't keep his mind from returning to Lindsay.

On second thought, he told himself, maybe he should tame that wolf and wish for amnesia. That might be the only way he'd forget her.

Feeling torn, miserable and caught in an uncustomary inability to make a decision, Lindsay stared at her dinner. She didn't want to eat but knew she should. Her thoughts were constantly on Tony. It seemed with each day she dreaded telling him about the baby more and more. She had to before she began to show and word got back to him. But when?

First she needed to go see Scotty, to hold him and think about having her own little baby, and then she needed to talk to Mike who would probably be a bulwark in the storm that would eventually rage around her. She didn't want to hide behind her brother from Tony, but Mike would take a levelheaded view of the situation and he and Savannah would support her in what she wanted to do.

Maybe she just needed to take Tony's call, go out with him and tell him the news. Get it over with and move on with her life and planning for her baby. Maybe Tony would back off and leave her alone.

She knew better than to expect that to happen. Mr. Take-Charge would dominate her life when she told him. Each time she thought of that happening, she was filled with dread.

She played with different scenarios in her mind: telling him soon, waiting four or five months to tell him or not saying a word until she had to. Like maybe when the baby was born.

As she headed to her house Friday afternoon, she was wrapped in worries and indecision and through it all, though she hated to admit it to herself, she missed Tony. She was so tired she paid little attention to her familiar surroundings until she steered her pickup toward the back of her house and saw a truck near the back gate. Frowning, she glanced at the house and saw Mike seated on the porch with his feet propped on the rail while he whittled.

She didn't know whether to be happy or annoyed with him and wondered whether Savannah had made him come.

As Lindsay parked behind his pickup and stepped out, Mike rose to his feet and put his knife away, along with whatever he had been whittling while he waited at the top of the steps. "What are you doing here?" she asked as she walked up the steps.

"Waiting to see if you need a big brother's hug," he said.

His kindness shook her and she walked into his arms. "I do," she whispered.

He hugged her, then stepped away to smile. "Let's go inside where we can talk and it's not a hundred degrees in the shade."

She tried to smile. "You mean where I can cry without

someone seeing me," she said, unlocking the door and leading the way. "Want a beer?"

"I'd like one, but not if it's going to make you want one."

"No. No problem there. I'll drink ice water." When they had drinks and were seated in the cool family room that overlooked the porch, patio and swimming pool, she sat facing him.

He had hung his hat on a hook in the entry hall and he raked his fingers through his hair. "Savannah said that you gave her permission to tell me." Mike leaned forward to place his elbows on his knees. "Here comes some brotherly advice and words of infinite wisdom."

She smiled. "There are moments I'm truly glad you're my big brother."

"I'm happy to hear that," he said. "There are moments I'm truly glad you're my little sis," he said, smiling at her. "Lindsay, don't forget for one minute that you have three brothers and three sisters-in-law who will support you in every way we can."

Tears threatened and she wiped her eyes. "Look at me, Mike. Do you know how few times in my life I've cried?"

"Chalk it up to hormone changes," he said. "I just want you to always remember you have our support and you can call me or Savannah anytime you want."

"Thanks. That means a lot," she said, meaning it with all her heart.

"Next thing—if being pregnant gets you down, just think of Scotty. You shower him with love and he seems to be a huge joy to you. He loves you and I know you love him. A baby in your life will be great."

"I know that and I do love Scotty beyond measure. He's adorable and I feel so close to him."

"He's a good kid. And he's going to love your baby. I

can promise you that. I'll let you tell Scotty when you're ready because he is very excited over Savannah's baby. He'll go into orbit over yours."

She smiled. "Maybe not so much if I have a girl."

"Oh, yes, he will. You wait and see. So now the next thing I want to mention, even if you don't want to hear it, is Tony. He's a good guy. I like Tony, and all the guys who work for him like him. All your brothers and sisters-in-law like him."

"I know that."

"Obviously, the two of you can get along. You were seeing each other after the auction."

"Does everyone in the state know we were going out together?"

"C'mon, Lindsay. All the Calhoun ranches and Milan ranches and the people that work on them—cleaning staff, cooks, cowboys—you think they don't get around and see who is leaving a ranch and who is entering one? Or talk about who they saw when they're out? The grapevine is alive and well in these parts. You and Tony were discreet about it, but your whole family probably knows you dated. Anyway, cut him some slack. He'll be shocked, but he's going to welcome this baby like I would, and you know it."

"Maybe that's what worries me. Tony is a take-charge guy."

Mike grinned. "I'm considering the source of that statement. Now, one last thing—would you like me to tell Mom and Dad before you talk to them?"

She thought about her parents and closed her eyes. She rubbed her hands together and looked at Mike. "Will Dad threaten Tony if he doesn't marry me? I haven't even wanted to think about dealing with our parents and, thank heavens, they're in California and have their own lives."

"Get some plans made before you tackle telling them. Tony's the one who has the difficult parents. Listen, all the rest of us will stand by you and between you and our folks. Mom will just have hysterics and faint."

Lindsay smiled and relaxed slightly. "Sounds ridiculous, but I think that might be exactly what she'll do. I've resisted her tears and hysterics plenty of times."

"The rest of us just hide from her. You're the brave one," he said, grinning. "Frankly, I don't think you'll have any pressure from our parents. They have their own lives, and I think when we grew up they let us go."

"I'm grateful for that. Tony is the person who worries me."

"You two will work it out." Mike squeezed her shoulder gently. He finished his beer and stood. "I've said what I wanted to say. I'll go home now. We're there for you—call in the middle of the night if you need us. You and Tony will work this out because you both love your families and you each will love this baby with all your hearts. You'll see."

"So when did you get to be such a counselor?" she said. Mike hadn't mentioned it, but she wondered if he or her other brothers would pressure her to marry Tony. "You know, even if we can be civil, Tony may not propose."

"There will probably be more than one pot for bets on that one," Mike remarked drily as they walked to the back door. Before they stepped outside, she closed her hand around his wrist.

"Thanks. Your advice might be a bit misguided, but your intentions are wonderful. You have cheered me up and I don't feel quite so alone."

"Lindsay, you should know your family well enough to know how very un-alone you are. Jake would be right here if you need him, or Josh. Tony's family will be the same." He stepped out on the porch, then resumed his talk. "There'll be plenty of kids on both sides of the family for your little one to bond with and to grow up with. Tony's sister, Madison, is pregnant. His brother Nick has a son, Cody, who is Scotty's age. I'll have another baby before yours is born. It'll be great." He reached out and gave her another hug.

"If only the father wasn't so take-charge and so stubborn."

"Said the kettle about the pot. You two are exactly alike in some ways and you're a strong enough woman to deal with most any man." He put his hat back on and made for the steps, then turned to her again. "Jake and Josh and I can go beat him up for you if you want."

"Mike, don't you dare!" He grinned and she saw he was teasing her. "Mike, shame on you, and I fell for it when I should know better."

"I made you smile," he said, sounding satisfied. "I gotta run, sis."

Lindsay followed him to his pickup. "Thanks for coming. I'll call Savannah and thank her. I liked her doctor—he was very nice, cheerful and kind. Now that I know for certain I'm pregnant, I'll have to find one around here. Savannah has one in Dallas she likes, so I'll probably get that name from her."

"When the time comes, you can stay at my house in Dallas if you want. If you stay on the ranch, you'll be a long way from your doctor and hospital."

"Thanks. We'll see."

"If you stay here, I guess it's a consolation that everyone on the place can probably deliver a baby."

"That's definitely not what I have in mind," she said

while she stood in the hot sun with her hands on her hips and stared at him.

"Call me and I'll do it." Grinning, he jumped into the truck and revved the engine.

"You're a wonderful brother, but you're not delivering my baby."

"For that matter, Tony can. He's good at delivering calves."

"Enough of you planning my life. How did I get tangled up with so many bossy men?"

"I think we're called alpha males," Mike corrected.

"Not in my view. I'll see you soon. Thanks for coming over."

"Sure." He smiled at her. "See you soon," he said, pulling along the driveway to head back to his ranch.

Smiling, she waved, but as the pickup drove out of sight leaving a plume of dust behind, her smile faded. None of Mike's cheerful advice or reminders of what a good guy Tony was changed the fact that Tony ran everything he could in his daily life. He was commanding, decisive, a Mr. Do-It-My-Way. Even as she enumerated those attributes, she felt a pain in her chest because she missed him. She ignored the feeling, certain it soon would stop haunting her and disappear forever.

She could tell him now, or she could tell him later. She was in for a fight and she felt it coming any which way she looked at her future.

Eight

Lost in thought, she walked into the house, mulling over how and when she would tell Tony.

By midnight she wasn't any closer to a solution. She sat in her darkened bedroom, looking out over her ranch and wondering what course of action she should follow. When the baby came, she would face more decisions. Stay home and take care of her baby all day or hire a nanny and go back to ranch work?

Eventually, she figured, that's probably what she would do, but she wanted to be home with her baby those first few months no matter what she decided to do later. Would she have to buy a house in Verity to secure a nanny or would she be able to find someone to live on the ranch? But maybe she was jumping the gun. First, she needed to find a doctor and have the baby.

She rubbed her forehead and thought about Mike's offer of his Dallas house in her ninth month. Tony might have some issue with that, being that he had a place in Dallas, too.

Tony. Mentioning his name made her remember he hadn't called her the past few days. Did he know she had been away from the ranch? She guessed he probably did, but he also knew she always had her phone. Had she heard the last from him until she contacted him?

On top of her worries and her woes, she missed Tony. He was too many wonderful things to suddenly have him disappear from her life and not feel his absence. She missed his energy, his optimism, his charm, his sexy ways. She didn't want to admit it, but a considerable amount of joy and excitement had gone out of her life. She dreamed about him at night, thought about him constantly during the day. Did Tony miss her at all?

The following Friday Tony climbed from his pickup after a long day. He'd helped some of his men clear a field. He was hot and dirty. He wanted a shower and a steak and he wanted to spend the evening with Lindsay. Since she hadn't taken his calls or answered his texts, he'd interpreted that as a sign she wanted to be left alone and he'd stopped calling. But that didn't stop him from wanting her.

He changed and went to his gym to work off the pent-up anxiety he felt from thinking about her. Exercising helped, as did swimming laps in his pool. But when he lay back in the pool, Lindsay invaded his thoughts once again. It was ridiculous, he told himself. If he didn't hear from her by next week, he promised himself he'd go out and forget all about her.

He swam laps until he couldn't stand to swim one more. Climbing out, he went in to shower and change, then work on taxes and his records. Later, he lay in the darkness, wanting sleep to come, hoping it was not another night of dreams filled with Lindsay.

During the night, he woke to hear a long, piercing howl. Stepping out of bed, he walked onto his balcony and gazed into the night. After a few minutes, another howl cut through the night. This one seemed to come from somewhere close to the barn nearest to his house.

Returning to his room, he pulled on his clothes and got a rifle. He went outside again to sit and wait, but the howls had stopped. He sat thinking about Lindsay, remembering times together, until he noticed the sky was getting lighter. It was dawn, so he went inside to shower and dress for the day.

After he had breakfast, he headed to the barn. Curious to see if he could find any signs of an animal, he knelt down and searched. But it was unlikely he'd find tracks in the hard, baked earth, so he rose and walked along slowly, studying the ground and turning a corner where thick bushes grew. He heard the faintest whine and froze for a minute. Then he moved slowly and cautiously toward the bushes, stopping instantly when he looked into a pair of brown eyes.

For a startled moment he thought it was a wolf, but then his gaze ran over the animal and he realized it was a big, furry gray-and-black male dog and it was hurt.

As the dog whimpered, Tony moved slowly, holding out his hand, wishing he had brought a piece of meat or something to offer. He spoke softly to the animal and knelt beside him. The dog tried to raise its head but lay back, watching him and giving one thump of its tail.

"Hey, boy," Tony said, speaking softly. "You're hurt." He saw the coat, tangled and matted with blood. One front leg and one hind leg each had bloody gashes. Tony pulled out his phone to call Keane.

* * *

Two hours later the dog was awake again, sedatives wearing off. Cleaned and bandaged, he lay in a stall in the barn on a blanket that had been tossed over hay spread on the floor. The barn was air-conditioned and comfortable.

Keane had helped Tony with the dog and, later, Doc Williams had stopped by. Now Tony was alone, sitting on the blanket by the dog and scratching its ears. He pulled out his phone and called Lindsay.

Warmth heated him at the sound of her voice. "I'm glad you answered."

"I've been in Dallas," she said, a cautious note in her voice that he'd never heard before.

He let her answer go without comment even though her phone had also been in Dallas. "Remember the howls and the coyote/wolf/dog?"

"Yes," she said, curiosity filling her voice so she sounded more like herself.

"He's in my barn. He was hurt, with lots of cuts. He may resemble a wolf, but he's actually just a big, furry gray dog that has been hurt. I thought you'd want to know."

"Oh, Tony, will he be all right?"

"Yes. Doc Williams has taken care of him. When the sedative completely wears off, he'll get a little steak. He's had some water. I held his head and sort of spoon-fed it to him. Want to come visit my patient?"

There was a pause. "Yes, I'll be there soon. Thanks for calling me. I'm headed to my pickup. By the way, how did you catch him?"

"I didn't catch him. He woke me in the night and when dawn came, I found him by the barn lying in the bushes where it was shady."

"I never thought about going to look for him. His

howling just gave me the creeps. But I'm so glad you rescued him. And it's a dog, huh?"

"Definitely. Mixed breed and looks like a wolf, but it's domesticated."

"It's wonderful that you saved him." He picked up the emotion in her voice.

"Well, well, Miss Tough Rancher is a real softie for dogs? How about men? Men named Tony?"

She laughed. "Maybe dogs."

He didn't press the point. He needed to slow down and just be happy that she'd taken his call. He brought the conversation back to the dog at his side. "Well, our patient already looks much better. Keane has a nice touch, and Doc said we did a good job. He said the dog has wounds from a fight. He's not sick, but Doc said he would stop by again and check on him."

"You're a good guy, Tony."

"I'm glad I can impress you," he said, brushing the dog's head as he talked. Despite his resolve, his eagerness to see Lindsay grew by the second. "We'll let you name him, Lindsay. Doc said no one had inquired about a lost dog that fit this one's description, and I've checked some ads and I don't see anything. I think he's homeless."

"I hope not any longer," she said breathlessly. "I hope you give him a home."

"We'll see how he fits in with the other dogs the guys keep on the ranch. I don't know what he's been fighting, but if he fights my dogs, I can't keep him."

"If you don't keep him, let me know." He heard her fumbling on the other end of the line, then she said, "I gotta go so I can drive."

"I'm in the first barn. Come on in."

"See you soon," she said and ended the call.

Putting away his phone, Tony smiled at the dog. He

was happy because Lindsay would soon be at his ranch. "Lindsay is coming to see you," he told the animal. "I hope she loves you and keeps coming to see you. Don't look too well too soon, okay, boy?"

The dog thumped its tail a few times. "I'll feed you in a while. Doc said to wait. Lindsay's going to love you and you're going to love her. Maybe you'll end up at her house and then I can come see you. Just be nice to all the ranch dogs. That's all that's required."

Big brown eyes looked up at him as the dog thumped his tail. Tony petted the dog's head gently, talking to it softly until he heard a motor. "Here she comes. Be a very nice dog now."

A pickup door slammed and Lindsay rushed in to stop in front of the stall. She had her hair in her usual braid and was in jeans and a blue T-shirt. She looked wonderful, and he fought the urge to get up, put his arms around her and kiss her.

"Hi, Tony. Oh, my, look at this beautiful dog," she said, coming into the stall to sit on the floor by Tony and reach out slowly to hold her hand in front of the dog, a treat in her palm.

He thumped his tail and raised his head slightly. His tongue licked out to take the treat.

"Oh, Tony, I'm so glad you didn't put him down. But he's all bandaged. Is he hurt badly?"

"Doc said he may limp. Other than that, he should heal just fine," Tony said, watching Lindsay instead of the dog. She smelled wonderful and she looked great. He still wanted to pull her into his arms and kiss her, but he knew that wasn't what she would want.

She placed her hand on the dog's head to pet him and he slowly thumped his tail.

"He has to get well. Thank you for calling me and

thanks for taking care of him. I think he's wonderful. Look at him. He's so sweet."

"You don't know if he's sweet yet. Remember, he still has the lingering effects of sedatives."

"He's sweet. You'll see. Look at those beautiful eyes."

"I am," Tony said, and she turned to look at him as he met her gaze.

She shook her head. "That's what I thought. You're not thinking about the dog."

"No, I'm not. It's good to see you."

She didn't respond to his statement. Instead, she teased him. "You know, if he had been a gray wolf, you could have had a wish granted, according to legend. As it is, you just became the owner of a stray dog."

"If I could have a wish, I'd wish that you'd go out with me tonight. But I guess, for the good of all, I would wish for rain this week."

"Doesn't matter. That was just a legend and he is just a dog." She petted him and Tony watched her. He couldn't help wishing those gentle hands were on his body, caressing him. But while her touch stilled the dog, it had aroused him.

"So," he prodded, "will you go out with me tonight?"

She turned to look at him solemnly, a slight frown on her brow, and he feared her answer. Then the frown disappeared and she nodded. "Tony, we need to talk," she said, suddenly sounding serious, as if she had something difficult to discuss. After her hesitation, she nodded again. "Yes. Tonight will be a big thank-you for rescuing this dog and giving him a home."

"Great. Let's go someplace fancy in Fort Worth. Someplace to dance, to talk and have a good time and super food, and then you can come back here and we'll see how our patient is doing."

Again he received a solemn look that puzzled him. "I don't know about coming back here, but we'll go out." Then, as if a thought just struck her, she asked, "But what about the dog? When you leave, he won't leave, will he?"

"I'll shut him in here where it's air-conditioned and he can be comfortable. In his condition, he can't get out. He'll have water and by that time I will have fed him something, so he should be all right."

"Do you want me to stay with him today?"

"Lindsay, I'm guessing you have a lot of things to do today."

She shrugged. "I suppose so, but I just don't want him to get up and go."

"He won't. I promise you."

She leaned down to croon to the dog and scratch behind his ears, and Tony took the opportunity to run his gaze over her. He didn't know if it was his imagination or just knowing what was beneath the clothes she wore, but she looked better than she used to with her braid, her old hat and jeans. Or was it because he hadn't seen her for a while and it was good to be with her again?

After a short time, she leaned back. "I need to get home, but I had to come see him."

They both stood and left the stall. While the dog raised its head, Tony closed the stall door and walked with Lindsay outside. "I'm glad you're going with me tonight. How about six so we have time to get to Fort Worth? I'll be glad to see you."

She smiled, but despite her acceptance of his dinner date, he sensed something off about her. Something had changed. There was a reluctance about her.

He tried to tease her out of her funk. "Still no fights between us, darlin'," he said quietly. "I'd say we've done well."

"Yes, we have, Tony. I hope it lasts," she said, and he had an even stronger feeling that something bothered her.

"Lindsay, come back into the barn for a minute."

She walked with him into the cool barn and turned to look at him with curiosity in her expression. "What's on your mind?"

"I wanted some privacy for us. Is anything wrong?"

Something flickered in her eyes and her cheeks became pink. "Not really. I just want to talk tonight."

He gazed into her eyes and wondered if he should probe more deeply. Then he figured they could talk tonight. But he couldn't let her go without doing one thing. When he stepped closer to place his hands on her shoulders, he felt her stiffen slightly. He studied her and then slipped his arm around her waist to kiss her.

"Tony, I should—" His lips on hers ended her talk.

For a moment she was resistant. Then all her stiffness vanished as she put her arms around his neck and returned his kiss passionately, a blazing kiss that meant whatever her problem was, she still couldn't cool the blazing sexual attraction between them.

When she stepped away, he let her go. She was breathing as hard as he was and they looked at each other a moment. Her blue eyes seemed clouded with worry. Turning away, she rushed out to her pickup.

"I need to get home, Tony. See you tonight," she called over her shoulder.

He hurried to watch her while she started the pickup. Gravely, she glanced at him and then drove away.

He stared after her. Something had definitely changed since the last time they were together. He didn't know what it was, unless she was trying not to tell him that she didn't care to go out with him again or receive phone calls from him. But knowing her as he did, he was certain she would have just said it.

That day was inevitable and he probably shouldn't have called her, but he knew she would want to see the dog. Oh, who was he kidding? He'd called because he wanted to see her. The dog was just an excuse. As much as he told himself to leave her alone and forget her, he couldn't stay away. His body seemed to crave her, the way a starving man craves food. Maybe tonight would be different, he told himself. Maybe tonight the reluctance and resistance he'd sensed in her would disappear. He could only hope.

He retrieved his hat and headed to his pickup to catch up with Keane and see how they were coming on clearing the land for the new pond.

But as he drove, he couldn't stop the niggling feeling that something big was going to happen tonight. Something sure as hell was wrong with Lindsay and he could only wonder what.

Lindsay spent the rest of the day at her house. Part of the time she helped her cook, Rosalee. Part of the time she was shut in her room deciding what to wear and how to tell Tony about her pregnancy.

She had wanted to wait, make her own decisions, but she couldn't go back to the carefree, happy times when she was with him after the auction. She had decided to tell him immediately and face dealing with him. It would come sooner or later and she wanted the battle over and done.

She wanted to look her best when she told him. When he was dazzled by her, Tony was much more cooperative. Take the night of the auction, for example. But then, that night she'd had surprise on her side. Oh, she had a surprise this time, all right. One that might make him faint.

Rummaging in her closet, she selected a black dress she had bought on impulse when she had been shopping in Dallas. She had never worn it, just because no occasion had arisen, but tonight should be one.

She yanked off her jeans to try on the dress. Before she pulled it on, she stopped to look at herself in the mirror. Even though it was too soon for physical changes, she couldn't keep from looking for them. It was satisfying to see she looked as slim as ever. Change was inevitable, but she hoped it didn't show really early. She wanted to keep working on the ranch, and if any of the guys noticed and realized, word would get to Abe. He would insist she stop and if she didn't, he'd probably talk to her brothers about it.

By five in the afternoon Rosalee had finished and left for the weekend. Lindsay had bathed and still worked to fix her hair, planning to leave it down in long spiral curls around her face.

As the time drew closer for Tony to arrive, her nerves became more raw. She dreaded talking to him, knowing all the peace between them would go up in flames tonight and they would each have to make a big effort to be civil and work out how they would deal with their new situation. Most of the changes would be in her life, but Tony would have adjustments and decisions, too. And their dates, their lovemaking, the fun they'd had—all that was over. It wasn't something she expected to get back in her life.

Feeling she had reached a point where her appearance was the best she could do, she went to the front window to watch for him coming up the drive. After a moment she stepped out on her porch to sit in a wooden rocker. In spite of the hot weather, she was chilled. Mounting dread about revealing her pregnancy to Tony enveloped her. She could anticipate his reactions and she suspected battles with him would fill the coming weeks. Underneath that dread was an undercurrent of anticipation, because she would finally be with him again.

When his sports car came into view, her pulse jumped. He might be bossy, but he still was the most charming, exciting, sexy man she had ever known. She went inside to take one more look at herself in the mirror, then stood waiting for the doorbell. Was she about to face her biggest struggle ever with Tony?

As Tony drove up the driveway to Lindsay's ranch house, his eagerness to see her grew. He'd been nervous all day to find out what disturbed her but, right now, knowing he'd see her in minutes, he couldn't help hoping for another hot, sexy night of lovemaking.

Never in his life had he been deeply involved in a serious relationship and he knew he wouldn't start now with Lindsay. They were just too different. Even so, at the moment he wanted to be with her; he missed talking to her and seeing her. He feared their tenuous relationship might be close to termination right now, but he intended to enjoy tonight to the fullest.

When the door swung open, his heart thudded and for seconds all he did was stare.

Lindsay wore another pair of stiletto heels with thin sexy straps crossing her slender feet, which matched her black sleeveless dress. Her plunging vee neckline revved his pulse another notch. Her straight, short skirt revealed her legs for him to view. Had she left her hair falling freely around her face to please him? Probably not, but he'd enjoy it anyway.

"You look gorgeous, Lindsay," he said. He was breathless, his voice deeper. "That black dress is killer on you."

She smiled at him, but it wasn't the wholehearted smile he had received before. "You've never been in my house. Come on in and look around."

He stepped in and the second he inhaled her perfume, he wanted to hold her and kiss her and forget about going out to dinner or eating anything for hours. He could cancel the reservations in Fort Worth and stay right here beside her.

He walked alongside her through a short hallway that opened out into a wide hall with a spiral staircase to the next floor. Above, a beamed ceiling was three stories high with skylights that let light pour into the house.

On either side of the stairs, the house opened up into spacious areas defined only by columns, furniture groupings and area rugs. The open rooms, high ceilings and lots of glass made the already large house seem twice as big.

"Like many other things about you, your house surprises me," he said. "It's beautiful, but not what I ever expected. I pictured you in a house more Western, but not the way you pictured mine would be. Just leather furniture and Western scenes in the paintings and traditional Western decor." He strolled into a living area he'd glimpsed from the hall and noticed a second-floor balcony extending over the length of one side of the room and the French period pieces upholstered in elegant silks and antique satins.

"Now I can picture you in your house," he said. "At least in part of it."

He turned to find her staring at him intently with a slight frown. Her expression jolted him. Just as he'd feared, something was very wrong and he didn't have a clue what it was.

"Lindsay, what's the problem?" he asked, unfastening the one button on his jacket and slipping out of it. He placed it on a chair. "Looks as if we need to talk."

As she wound her fingers together, her knuckles whitened. He took her hands in his.

"The weight of the world might as well be on your shoulders. Whatever is bothering you can't be that bad." He bent his knees so he could look directly into her eyes. Silently, he studied her.

"Before we talk, I think it would be wise to cancel our dinner reservation. I debated just telling you to come over for dinner, but I thought I might not have the courage to talk to you tonight—"

"Damn, Lindsay, what the hell? Is it—"

"Don't start guessing. Cancel the dinner reservation. My cook was here today and I had her leave us a casserole if either of us feels like eating later."

Watching her, he pulled out his phone, looked down and sent a short text. He put away his phone.

"I think you might like a drink. I'll get you a beer," she said.

Mystified, he stared after her. Whatever this was, the problem disturbed her a hell of a lot more than any other she'd encountered while he'd known her. From the way she was acting, it seemed even catastrophic.

Was it the ranch? Did she have to sell it? If she did, she wouldn't have any trouble telling him. Nor could it involve anyone in her family; he didn't think she would hesitate letting him know that.

He knew she had gone to Dallas recently. He also realized she had another life away from her ranch. Was it someone else? Did she have a lover in Dallas? No, she wouldn't have stayed with Tony if there'd been anyone else.

So why did she go to Dallas? Did she have some illness and need a big-city doctor?

She looked as healthy as anyone could hope to be, even though that was no indication of how she might feel or why she would have to see a doctor. The thought that Lindsay was sick was like a punch to his middle. What was wrong and how serious was it? Was it incurable? That question almost buckled his knees.

He watched her behind the bar fixing their drinks and went to join her. The more he thought about it, the more convinced he was that she had gone to Dallas because of a medical problem. She knew when she told him he'd need a drink.

What the hell could be so wrong that she knew ahead of time and it involved him enough for her to expect him to be upset?

His knees did almost cave on that one. He sat on the nearest bar stool while he stared without seeing anything and his head spun.

One possibility occurred to him and he knew in every inch of his being that he guessed correctly. Taking deep breaths, he looked up to see her coming around the bar with a glass of ice water for herself and a whiskey on the rocks for him.

"I thought you might prefer this," she said, handing him his drink. She frowned. "Tony, you look white as a sheet."

"You're pregnant, aren't you? You're carrying my baby."

Nine

"How did you find out?"

He closed his eyes. "Wow," he whispered. "I just figured it out. I tried to think of reasons for you to go to Dallas. And reasons for the big change in you since the way you were with me before you went to Dallas. And when you offered to get a drink for me, I realized it had to involve me, too. There was only one thing I could think of." He reached for the drink she held out. "I think I need that whiskey now."

He downed it in one swallow and set down an empty glass. "I'm in shock. You're going to have to give me a minute to digest this bit of news," he said. "You've had time to think about it a little."

He sat there staring at the floor but not seeing anything, just thinking about the changes coming in his life—changes that would be monumental.

He would be a father. Lindsay would have his child.

He was so dazed he knew he couldn't even fathom the changes that would downright transform his life. He couldn't even try.

There would be no financial worries for either one of them, so he could cross that concern off his list. But there was one giant problem—and only one solution.

He pulled himself together as best he could and stood up to take her hand.

"Lindsay, marry me."

His words didn't have the desired effect. Instead, he watched a transformation come over her and he had a sinking feeling a proposal wasn't what she wanted. Once again her stubbornness surfaced. He could see that in the set to her jaw and the fire in her eyes. Annoyance filled him as it always had. From the start he had known she always stirred up conflict, and this was no exception.

"Tony, that's a knee-jerk reaction. You take some time and think this through. I'm financially well-fixed, so that's not a consideration. I have a big, supportive family, so I'll have all the help I need. The biggest reason I can't marry you is that we are basically not compatible." Before he could make a point, she added, "You're bossy and arrogant and you want to take charge of every situation—which is exactly what you're doing right now. I don't want you telling me what to do."

Impatience stabbed him. Every issue was a conflict with her. Why did he think for one second this wouldn't be? She was, as always, her usual stubborn self. But then his gaze roamed over her and for an instant he forgot everything. She was stunning. Even steeped in worry, when he looked at her, she took his breath away.

"Lindsay, stop and think and consider my proposal. Don't answer now. It's the logical solution for a lot of reasons, plus we get along great in some ways."

With a slight frown, she started to answer, and he placed his finger on her soft lips. "Shh. Don't answer me now—give my proposal time and think of all the positive reasons to do this. We can be compatible, we have these big families that have drawn close and we'll be thrown together constantly. All you're thinking about right now is that I'm a rancher and how I run my ranch. Just think of all the things in our lives and give my offer consideration." He walked behind the bar to pour another drink. He stood there, not saying a word, sipping the whiskey while she was quiet. He suspected she was getting her argument lined up.

Shock still reverberated in him. Of all people—Lindsay would have his baby.

Everything fell into place—why she didn't want to see him, why she was so somber. He walked to the window with his back to Lindsay and the room and stared outside. His entire life was about to change drastically. After a few moments he turned around to find her still standing where he had left her. She looked at him but said nothing.

His mind reeled with questions. He gave one voice. "When did you find out?"

She told him. "As soon as I realized I was late, I had a feeling. I went to a doctor and had the lab work done. I wanted to confirm it before I told you."

He nodded. "This is something I thought would never happen—an unplanned pregnancy. I know you thought the same thing."

They lapsed into silence again as he contemplated the changes coming in his life. Fatherhood. Coming fast and unexpected.

"Did you get a doctor in Dallas? I assume that's why you went."

"No. I know too many people there. I called Savannah

and got an appointment with her doctor in Little Rock. I didn't want word to get back to you until I could tell you myself. I didn't think about you guessing correctly."

"Well, you'll have to find a doc closer than Little Rock," he remarked drily. "Damn."

"I will. I just couldn't take a chance going to any big Texas city where I could have run into someone I know."

Another silence fell and he was thankful again that she was giving him a chance to adjust to his new status before they talked very much.

"There are a few things I think we can decide tonight."

As he stared at her, he thought, *Here we go*. She sat at the edge of a pale antique satin sofa and crossed her legs. Long, beautiful legs—the best pair of legs he had ever seen. As he looked at her, he noted that her blond hair was like a halo around her head. In almost every respect, he knew this woman would be the best mother possible for his child. He just hadn't planned on fatherhood so soon. And he and Lindsay were not in love. She didn't like ranchers. He didn't like her stubborn streak, her knack for constantly living in conflict.

"We should keep this between us for a little longer, if possible," he said, "until we make some major decisions about the future."

She nodded. "When people hear I'm expecting a baby, I'm going to get questions."

"That's fine with me. Whatever you want. You said Savannah knows and, I'm assuming, Mike. Who else?"

"Besides you, no one else. Believe me, Mike and Savannah know how to keep quiet."

"Good. It's better for both of us to keep it quiet for now," he repeated. "You don't show at all and I doubt if you will for another month. That gives us time." He became silent, his thoughts swirling in his head. Like a mantra, one statement kept reverberating in his mind. Lindsay was pregnant with his baby.

His gaze swept over her again. She was the most beautiful woman he had ever known. And the sexiest. He remembered their lovemaking, which was never out of his thoughts long. Marriage to her would have big pluses, if her stubbornness didn't overshadow the rest.

She'd had a bit of time to think about this and adjust to the prospect of being pregnant, so she might have already made decisions about the future. He'd better come out of shock and plan what they should do.

Minutes ticked past while he tried to sort through the jumble of thoughts, possibilities and outcomes. Finally, her voice broke the silence.

"I never thought this would be a problem I'd have," she said, gazing up at him. Her blue eyes were wide and clear.

"There's a simple solution I've already given you." She directed a steady look at him and he could feel the battles looming between them. "Lindsay, we're going to have a baby," he said. "You know I'll love this baby with all my heart."

"I know you will," she replied.

"Did the doctor tell you an approximate due date?"

"Next May."

"Then we should have that wedding soon," he said, and her eyes flared.

"I'll do what I feel I have to do," she said, the old tension coming between them again. He could feel the first stir of his own anger over her answer. Trying to curb it, reminding himself of the huge upheaval this would cause in her life, he crossed the space between them to draw her to her feet and place his hands on her shoulders. She stiffened.

He could feel barriers coming up between them. Anger

plagued him over her stubborn refusal to cooperate, which showed in her body language as well as her facial expression.

But who was he kidding? In spite of the problems and differences between them, he still wanted her—in his arms, in his bed. The minute he touched her, that familiar desire flared up in every part of him, and if he wasn't mistaken, he caught the same response in her.

Unable to resist any longer, he pulled her into his arms to kiss her hard and passionately. For an instant she pushed against him, but he couldn't step away if he wanted to, and in seconds, her arm went around his neck and she surrendered to his kiss. It was all the invitation he needed.

In one motion he peeled away her black dress while he continued to kiss her. When her bra was gone, he caressed her breasts, kissing first one and then the other. Her moans and soft breaths encouraged him to take her. He paused only long enough to strip off his clothes. Then, naked and hard, he picked her up and lowered her onto the sofa. Without a second's hesitation he entered her in one smooth thrust. She was ready for him. Hard and fast, they moved together. Quickly, desperately, she clutched him to her as she climaxed with him, her cries muted by his frantic kisses. They both gasped for breath as wave after wave of ecstasy washed over them.

For Tony, though it was fast and furious, this was the best lovemaking he'd ever had. He leaned back to tell her as much till he saw the look in her eyes. He'd expected a contented haze; instead, he found a storm brewing in their blue depths.

She stared at him and he could feel her anger rising again.

Instead of lashing out, she simply pushed him off her.

"I'm going to shower, Tony. I'll be back shortly," she said, still breathless. She yanked up her clothes and left.

He watched her walk away and wondered if he could ever get her to listen and cooperate or if they were at an impasse. Gathering his clothes, he went to find a bathroom and dress. As he did, his thoughts were on Lindsay. Would she even talk to him when she came back?

He returned to wait and soon she entered the room. As always, she made his heart beat faster. "You look gorgeous."

She had changed from her dress and wore a white linen blouse and white slacks with white high-heeled sandals and she still looked good enough to model.

"Thank you," she said in a dismissive manner, as if she barely heard what he had said. "Tony, I think our evening is over. I don't feel like dinner together."

He tried to curb the flash of anger that returned. Stubborn, stubborn woman who wanted life her way and her way only.

He wouldn't leave, not without reiterating his proposal. "Lindsay, the logical thing is for us to get married. Think about it tonight."

"I will," she said, but from the way she replied, with anger in her voice, he suspected the next time he saw her, he would get only arguments about marrying.

She raised her chin. "Do you really think we can get along in day-to-day living?"

They stared at each other and he felt the palpable clash of wills.

"See. I proved my point," she said. "Frankly, Tony, I'm trying to hang on to my temper. I really would like to scream at you for getting me pregnant, except I know full well that I had as much part in that happening as you did."

"Thank you for that one." At least she was rational. "Lindsay, I just see one solution and I hope you'll come to the same conclusion."

"We irritate each other."

"Sometimes, but we can get past the problems. I know now that beneath the tough rancher is a stunning, sexy woman who can simply melt me."

"Tony," she said impatiently, "whatever we found compatible in the past few weeks since the night of the auction… it's gone. That's over."

"Not altogether," he remarked drily. "We found it again less than an hour ago."

Anger flashed in her expression. She closed her mouth tightly while she glared at him.

"I know we need to work this out," she said after a few minutes of silence. "I just can't be the same person with you that I was."

"Don't stop communicating. I won't be cut off from my child. I want this baby in my life and I feel strongly that, if possible, a baby needs both a mom and a dad. That isn't always feasible, but in this case, it damn sure is, Lindsay," he said, trying to keep his temper.

Again, he got a glacial stare. "I know it, Tony. We both caused this and I agree that we both need to be in our baby's life. But don't pressure me," she snapped.

"Dammit, Lindsay. Before you make any decisions, stop and think about our baby. I'll talk to you later." He walked out before he lost it with her.

He slammed the door and hurried to his car, then drove away. Had she already closed her mind to his proposal?

Lindsay felt as if all the frustration and anger building in her since realizing she was pregnant had finally burst and she couldn't act as if nothing had changed between them.

His controlling personality had surfaced in a big way tonight—a glimpse of what she would live with if she even considered his proposal. She couldn't imagine being married to him and taking orders from him every day.

She hadn't been able to resist his kisses, succumbing to sex, but afterward she regretted the intimacy. Sure, there was no doubt they were sexually compatible but, as she'd said many times, sex wasn't everything. Outside the bedroom, she couldn't live with him.

She had wanted him to leave. She wanted to tell him goodbye and not see him again until she worked things out for her future.

One thing her feelings were certain about was that she was not going to marry Tony. That would be disastrous for both of them.

Just as she'd expected, he had tried to take over her life tonight. In marriage he would take over her ranch, tell her what to do on a daily basis. Besides, they weren't in love.

She could imagine Tony wanting to put both ranches together with him running everything while she stayed home to raise their child. That wasn't going to happen.

In spite of her irritation with him, when she looked at the sofa, she saw Tony there, his marvelous, strong body, his vitality, his sexy lovemaking that still now made a tremor run through her. But it was over.

Though she was too upset to sleep, she got ready for bed and sat in a chair in the dark, her eyes adjusting to the moonlight that spilled into her bedroom.

Knowing she should go to bed but certain she would just stare into the darkness and sleep would still escape her, she sat where she was until she finally fell asleep in her chair.

When she crawled into bed, it was almost four in the morning. As soon as her head touched the pillow, memories of better moments with Tony bombarded her. Then she thought about tonight with him and felt her anger return.

The next day she sent a text to Abe that she couldn't work. She needed to tell him about her pregnancy, but she had to get a grip on her emotions. When she talked to Abe, she had to be able to tell him that she had decided to turn the daily running of the ranch over to him, and she had to be able to say it without tears. She loved her ranch, working on it, raising her horses, dealing with livestock and making decisions. Her land was beautiful to her, spreading endlessly to a blue horizon with gorgeous sunrises and sunsets. Tony wasn't going to marry and take that away from her.

She had been nauseated after breakfast this morning and she wondered if that was something she would have every morning. She needed to find a Dallas doctor, as well as decide where she would live in her ninth month.

Three days later she still hadn't told Abe anything except that she couldn't work. Soon he would come to see about her, but she dreaded telling him. He could keep it quiet, that she could count on. But him knowing just made it more real.

She tried to do some of her paperwork, but she couldn't keep her mind on it. There was no call from Tony, but that didn't surprise her. What did surprise her was how much she missed him.

She sat staring into space and thinking about Tony. If she wouldn't marry him, would it hurt when he married later? Would she be able to watch him go out of her life except when it was necessary to see him because of their child?

She hadn't considered that before and it hurt to think of Tony marrying someone else. If the thought of Tony marrying hurt, how much did she really care for him? Could she be in love with him?

No way she could be in love with him. He was too authoritative, too opinionated, so certain he was always right. There was a point where all her affection and his appeal came to a stop.

They would have their lives tied together for years to come, but going out with each other the way they had been had ended. She saw that clearly and felt it was for the best. Just as swiftly, she felt a pang at the thought of not going out with him, of not making love to him. Startled, she shook her head. Life with Tony was over and that was the way she wanted it. She would stop missing him soon.

And what about Tony? He might want out of seeing her just as much. He had been in shock last night. The proposal had been a knee-jerk reaction. Now that he was home to think things through alone, his conclusions about the future might have changed.

The idea made her feel even more forlorn, as if she were losing someone important. As the day passed, she tried unsuccessfully to shake the feeling of loss. How long would it be before she stopped missing him?

Ten

As each day passed, Tony tried to adjust to the situation. Without thinking, too often he reached for his phone to call Lindsay only to stop himself. He'd reminded himself how mulish she could be. But that didn't stop him from missing her.

Friday afternoon, the second of October, when he returned from work he saw Lindsay's pickup on his drive.

His heart jumped and he sped up his steps, all tiredness leaving him instantly. Lindsay stepped out of her pickup and his breath caught in his throat. She wore tight jeans, a clinging red T-shirt with a vee neckline. Her hair was in the usual braid and she had a wide-brimmed brown hat on her head. She looked great to him and his pulse raced as eagerness to talk to her made him walk even faster.

"Hi," he said as he approached, smiling.

She gave him a fleeting smile and he drew a deep

breath because she kept a wall between them. He could feel her coolness toward him and knew there was a specific reason for her visit.

"Come in, Lindsay."

"No, I just thought I'd stop in and talk in person instead of on the phone, but this won't take long. Now that my waist is getting a bit bigger—"

He looked down at her and wondered if she could even be one inch larger. "You don't look it."

"I feel it. Anyway, as I was saying, now that I'm getting bigger, I want to tell my family that I'm pregnant and I want to tell Abe and the guys."

"Lindsay, have you even thought about our baby?"

Her eyes narrowed and her cheeks flushed. He was certain she would start yelling at him any minute. He struggled to keep his temper.

"Yes, I have," she said. "I still don't want to marry you. You would want to take charge of every detail of my life and of our child's upbringing. Hell, no, I'm not marrying you."

"You're so damn stubborn, you'd mess up your own life."

"It still is my 'own life.' Are you okay with telling our families? I'll just tell them that we're working out our plans. They'll accept what I tell them."

"That's probably a good idea, because you need to get a doctor and word has a way of spreading, especially when it's about babies. I'll tell my family, too. And Keane and the guys. And I'll tell all of them I asked you to marry me and you said no—but that opens you up to some pressure."

"No more than I'll get anyway." She opened the door to her pickup. "Thanks, Tony. We got that settled."

He put his hand on her door and blocked her way from climbing in.

"It doesn't have to be this way."

"I don't see how things can be any other way," she said. He dropped his hand and held the door for her while she climbed in.

"Bye," he said as he closed the door, feeling as if this was a real and lasting farewell. That any intimacy or closeness they'd shared—the laughter and joy and steamy sex—all of it was over. Stepping away, he rested his hands on his hips as he watched her drive away, heading back to the county road to go home to her ranch. As her pickup widened the distance between them, he knew he would always remember the day she drove out of his life. He didn't think they would ever be close again. A cloud of gloom, along with his anger, settled on him as he entered the house.

The following week, Tony saw he had a text from his sister, Madison; she wanted to come see him. With a sigh he sent her a text in return.

Yes, you can come see me. Tonight's fine. Tomorrow morning is fine. Take your pick or suggest a time.

They had finally settled on early Saturday. He waited on the porch because it was a cool, sunny morning.

He watched Madison come up the walk. Her brown hair was in a ponytail. She wore jeans and a tan cotton shirt that was not tucked into her jeans. In spite of hiding her waist, it was obvious she was months along in her pregnancy. He placed his arm around her shoulders to give her a brief hug, then led her inside the house. "Haven't seen you in a while. I have breakfast ready. Or anything else you'd like."

"I've had breakfast. I'll just have a glass of ice water. It's a beautiful morning and what is even more wonderful is that rain is predicted next week—they give it a twenty-percent chance."

"If it actually happens, I'm going out to just stand in it. Might take a picture of it since it's been so long since I've seen any."

She smiled. "Is Gwynne here?"

"Not on Saturday. How are you feeling?"

"Fine. Just bigger by the day." She faced him, her green eyes sparkling. "Tony, congratulations. I've talked to you on the phone, but I wanted to tell you in person. I'm so happy for you and Lindsay. I know you have things to work out, but you will. A baby is so wonderful."

"Thanks, Madison. It's sort of a mixed blessing at this point in my life."

"It's an enormous blessing. And our babies will not be so far apart in age," she said, rubbing her stomach lightly.

"I can't think that far ahead," he remarked drily. "I'm just getting accustomed to this becoming-a-dad business."

She laughed and accepted the glass of water as he handed it to her. "I'll carry your coffee, Tony," she said as he helped himself to scrambled eggs from a pan on his stove. He added a piece of ham and picked up a slice of toast.

"I'm set. It's beautiful outside. Let's sit on the porch."

As soon as they were seated at a glass-topped iron table, he sipped his coffee and sat in silence, certain she had a mission.

"Tony, any chance you want some sisterly advice?"

"Actually, no," he said, smiling at her, "but since this drive to visit me was unprecedented and a little difficult for you under the circumstances, I'm sure I'm going to get some."

"I'm just concerned. And Jake is concerned about his sister. She's hurting, and I came to see for myself how you're faring."

"I'm faring fine," he said, startled to hear about Lindsay. He'd figured she had gotten on with her life and wasn't giving much thought to him. He knew she had stopped working with the men.

"Mike Calhoun's wife is expecting her baby this month, which is exciting. We'll have the three new babies, plus Cody and Scotty. Our families are growing and I think it's exciting and wonderful."

He smiled at her. "At the moment, you're in love with Jake, having his baby, and the whole world looks rosy to you," he said, studying her and realizing she looked happier and prettier than ever before.

"You're right," she agreed. "Are you okay?"

"I'm absolutely fine. And you're looking good yourself. I think marriage and motherhood really suit you."

"I'm happy, Tony. So happy with Jake," she said.

"Our dad should have stayed out of your lives and not deceived you about Jake, as well as driving him away," Tony said quietly. "I don't know how you can ever forgive him. Dad and I have butted heads since I was able to talk back to him. I paid for it, but I never got along with him the way Wyatt and Nick did."

"Wyatt is quiet and peaceful. Nick's the politician who's going to please the world and he started by pleasing Dad. And I always, well, until high school, did what he wanted. I never dreamed he would interfere in my life the way he did." Her frown disappeared and she smiled. "That's over. Jake and I are married, having a baby and I'm happier than I ever dreamed possible." Impulsively, she reached out to squeeze her brother's hand. "I hope you find that with Lindsay, Tony. You can't imagine how wonderful marriage can be."

He laughed. "I do believe you're in love, sis. That's good. You and Jake deserve all the happiness in the world. I'm amazed Jake hasn't punched Dad out."

"Jake isn't going to hit an elderly man, much less hit my father."

"He has a right to."

"Whatever," she said, flipping back her hair. "Anyway, I'm glad to hear you're okay. I just wanted to see for myself. I'm excited our babies will be fairly close in age. December and May aren't really far apart after the first year or two."

"Madison, you didn't drive out here to tell me how thrilled you are about our babies being close in age. You could have done that on the phone."

"Well, I more or less did. And to see if you're okay."

"I'm quite okay. But what's wrong with Lindsay?"

"I think she's just unhappy."

"Well, Jake should realize that being pregnant has put a big crimp in her lifestyle. For corn's sake, look how she's always lived—like one of the guys. Suddenly, she's a woman and her body has limitations because of her pregnancy. She's not accustomed to that, didn't expect it and evidently is having difficulty adjusting to it."

"Just be nice to her, Tony. It's a big change and for Lindsay, without a husband, without planning for a baby, changing her entire life and future is an enormous upheaval."

"She'll adjust. And she could have a husband if she wanted," he said, unable to keep the bitterness out of his voice. "She turned me down absolutely. Lindsay will handle this just like she handles everything else—in full control."

"You think a lot of her, don't you?" Madison asked.

"Sure, I do. Every rancher in the area does. She's capable and intelligent."

"You didn't take her out because she's capable and intelligent."

He laughed. "No, she can be fun and pretty."

"Lindsay has the looks of a model when she wants to. I saw her at the auction. Anyway, you be nice to her. She needs you now."

"I'll be nice to Lindsay," he said with amusement. "Though I don't think she needs me or wants to see me or talk to me."

Madison sat quietly so long that he turned to look at her. "What?" he asked.

She stood. "I've seen that you're doing fine. I don't want to pry into your life with Lindsay. I just want you to know that I'm excited about your baby. I should go home now."

"That was a short visit, but I'm glad you came. Madison, let me know when Mike's baby is born. I might not hear about it."

"Lindsay will tell you," she said.

"Lindsay isn't going to tell me one damn thing."

Madison looked startled and stared at him intently.

"We don't speak, we don't see each other. It'll have to change later, but that's the way she wants it now."

"Sorry to hear that. I'll tell you about Mike and Savannah." She gave him a hug, then leaned away to look intently at him again. "Be patient with Lindsay. This is a giant change for both of you."

"Sure," he answered, knowing his sister meant well. He stood on the porch and watched her drive away, his thoughts on Lindsay. Lindsay was unhappy? She did what she wanted to do.

And how unhappy was she? It had to be a lot to worry Jake enough to get Madison to drive out and talk to him. He wished Lindsay's unhappiness was because she missed him, but he knew better. She was probably unhappy with him and unhappy she had to change her lifestyle.

He carried his dishes into his empty house. As he passed his landline, he stared at the phone, tempted to pick it up and call Lindsay to just talk. He missed her and every time he realized that he missed her, it surprised him.

How important had she become to him?

He couldn't answer his own question.

The next week he threw himself into work, going to the corral to ride some of the unbroken horses at night with a few of the men who worked for him, just keeping busy. But none of it stopped the moments of longing for Lindsay.

Nights were long and unpleasant. He had always fallen into bed and been asleep instantly, sleeping soundly until early morning. Not anymore. His nights were filled with memories of Lindsay, dreams about her, moments of missing her.

The weekends were worse because he had no one he wanted to go out with. He missed her and the longing to see her intensified instead of diminished, until he finally sat up in bed one night, tossed back the covers and walked out on his porch.

The gray dog was still recovering, but better. The bandages were gone and his hair, where they'd had to shave it away to work on his cuts, was growing out again. He had gained weight and his coat was shiny now. Tony kept it brushed so it wasn't a tangle.

Tony let him stay at the house with him. The dog

seemed a faint tie to Lindsay, and Tony enjoyed having him around. When he went to the porch, the dog followed him, sitting with his head on Tony's knee while Tony scratched his ears. "Maybe I should invite her over to see you," he said to the dog, who wagged his bushy tail.

Tony sat quietly while he thought about Lindsay. He thought about her constantly each day. Was he in love with her and hadn't realized it when it happened?

If he was, he didn't know where it could lead. She was as stubborn as ever, refusing to give an inch, while she had accused him of being too take-charge and bossy. Plus, he was a rancher—the kind of man she said she would never marry.

He sat in the dark and mulled over his feelings for Lindsay and the problems between them.

Madison had said Lindsay was unhappy. Was their parting a cause of her unhappiness? Could he ever get past her stubborn nature? He had some of the time. His heartbeat quickened at the thought of getting past their problems. Could he think before he told her what she should do?

Could he live without her?

Was he in love with her?

Staring into the dark, he realized he was. He wanted her in his life. Lindsay would be a challenge, but if he loved her, he would cope with her. But could he get her to consider working with another rancher? That wasn't impossible. He worked with them all the time and for that matter, she did, too.

Suddenly feeling better, he wanted to call her and he wanted to be with her. One thing he knew for certain: he didn't want to lose her. Someone would come along and marry her and, at the thought, he felt as if he had been punched in his heart.

He needed to get her a ring and tell her how he felt and propose—for real this time. He had fallen in love with her and hadn't even recognized the depth of his own feelings.

He remembered her call at three in the morning when the dog was howling. It was about four o'clock now. What would happen if he called her, told her he had to see her? Could he get her to listen to him and go out with him?

Or was she out of his life no matter what he felt for her?

Lindsay sat up and shook her hair back away from her face. She stared into the dark bedroom as she clutched the phone. "Tony?" she asked, sounding more alert. "It's four in the morning. What's wrong?"

"Lindsay, I need to see you. Let me pick you up for dinner tonight."

She frowned at the phone. "You called at 4:00 a.m. to ask me to dinner?"

"You called at three to tell me a dog was howling. Will you have dinner with me? We need to talk."

She couldn't imagine what the urgency was, but her heartbeat quickened because she missed him and she wanted to be with him.

"Yes, I'll go to dinner with you. But you do know I'm pregnant and need my sleep, right?"

"I figured four is close enough to when you'll get up anyway. And can't you go back to sleep?"

"Yes," she said, but she wondered whether she would or not.

"Me, too, darling'," he said, and a warm fuzziness filled her. She hadn't heard that endearment in too long and it made it worth the wake-up call. "How about I pick you up at six?" he asked.

"That's fine," she said, curious what was on his mind.

"See you then," he said, and was gone.

She settled in bed, turning toward the windows so she could look at the bright moonlight outside. White cumulus clouds drifted rapidly across the black sky. She missed Tony more than she would have believed possible. She missed him every day and thought about him constantly and got lost in memories too often each day.

When had Tony become so important to her? At first she'd thought she would forget him as the days passed. Instead, each day she missed him and thought of him more.

She hadn't faced the question that hovered in her mind. Was she in love with him? Had she fallen in love with a man who would always want to run her life, their child rearing and her ranch? All indications said she had. She didn't know his feelings for sure, but she knew he hadn't been in love with her when she last saw him.

Tony had been so many good things—energetic, sexy, positive and upbeat, full of fun and life. She knew he was a good rancher. And she knew he was a take-charge person. Could she cope with having him back in her life? And on a larger scale? She couldn't answer her own question. The only solid answer she could give was that she had been miserable without him. She didn't want to tell him goodbye and watch him marry another woman while she raised his child.

This time without Tony had been the unhappiest stretch in her life. Excitement coursed through her at the thought of seeing him again. What was so urgent that he had to see her tonight? She hoped it was to get back together. She didn't know how they could, but she was ready to try.

She climbed out of bed, moving restlessly to a chair to think about Tony. She was guessing he wanted to see her because he missed her, too. But what if he had another reason—like a permanent parting of the ways?

That possibility filled her with concern. It couldn't happen now, she told herself, not when she finally realized she wanted him back in her life with all her being.

He still might propose to her again, even if he didn't love her. If he did, was she willing to accept that and hope she could win his love over time?

She ran her hand across her flat stomach. Their baby needed them. Could they set aside their monumental differences and give love a chance?

There was love on her part. She was ready to admit it now. She was in love with Tony, alpha male or not. She had gotten herself into this situation by bidding on him at the auction, and now she was in deep, over her head.

Would she tell him that she was in love? Or keep it from him until he declared feelings of love for her? She didn't see how she could keep from revealing her love to him. At the thought of seeing him tonight, what she most wanted was to throw herself into his arms when she opened her door. Now that she knew she would see him and had finally admitted that she was deeply in love, she ached to be with him and hoped with all her heart he might have missed her or, better yet, be as in love as she was.

She glanced at her clock and saw it was almost five. In just over twelve hours she would be with him and get an answer to the question that plagued her. What did Tony feel for her?

Only time would tell.

By six that night she had even more questions. As she left her room, she turned for one more look in the mirror. She wore a deep blue sleeveless dress with a low-cut back, a hem that ended above her knees and high heels. She had left her hair falling freely because Tony liked that best.

Downstairs, promptly at six she watched him step out of his black sports car and come up her front drive, and her breath rushed from her lungs. He looked handsome, filled with vitality. He also looked like a Texas rancher in his white Stetson, his black boots, black Western-cut trousers and a pale blue, long-sleeved cotton shirt that was open at the throat. She longed to throw herself into his embrace, but she restrained herself, opening the front door and smiling.

His blue-green eyes filled with desire that revved up her heartbeat. "Darlin', you look gorgeous," he said, his gaze moving over her slowly, a tantalizing perusal that set her pulse pounding. "You look more fantastic than ever. I'd say that pregnancy becomes you."

"Thank you. I'd say prospective fatherhood becomes you, because you're a sexy hunk, Tony Milan." As she spoke she was unable to keep from letting her gaze skim over him, wanting more than ever to be in his arms and kiss him.

"Lindsay," he said.

She looked up to meet his hungry gaze and her heart thudded at the heat and desire she saw there. He stepped inside and closed the door. She didn't have to throw herself into Tony's arms. He drew her into them and kissed her.

Her heart slammed against her ribs and she clung to him to kiss him in return. "Tony, I've missed you," she whispered breathlessly between kisses.

"I'm not doing any of this the way I planned," he said, between showering her with kisses.

Looking into his eyes, she felt a physical impact that

heated her insides. It seemed months instead of weeks since she last saw him.

He kissed her and she closed her eyes again, holding him tightly while her heart pounded.

"I might not let you go this time," he whispered. He showered kisses on her and finally picked her up, carrying her as he kissed her. "We were going to my house, but I think that's temporarily on hold. This is far too urgent," he said. "Lindsay, I've really missed you."

Clutching his shoulders, she kissed him slowly and thoroughly. "I've missed you."

He took the stairs two at a time, hurrying to the big bed in her room.

It was covered with dresses, lacy underwear, bits and pieces of clothing that she had tried on earlier.

He yanked back the cover and all of the clothing flew off. He turned to kiss her, his fingers trembling as he drew the zipper of her dress down while she twisted free the buttons of his shirt. She couldn't wait to show him how much she loved him.

Over an hour later, she lay wrapped in his arms beside him in bed while he lightly combed her hair away from her face with his fingers and showered feathery kisses on her temple and cheeks.

"I think we were going to my place for dinner," he whispered, nuzzling her neck and kissing her throat so lightly.

"We still can if you want or I can find something here to feed you."

"I had plans and I wanted to show you the dog."

She sat up so fast he rolled away slightly. "The dog? You didn't tell me. Is he okay?"

"He's more than okay," Tony said, smiling as he pulled

her back against his shoulder and held her close. "Lindsay, I've missed you, darlin', more than I thought possible and I've thought about my feelings for you."

She focused on him, her heart beginning to drum, and she could barely catch her breath upon hearing his words. He gazed into her eyes and looked at her intently. "Lindsay, I love you."

"Oh, Tony," she gasped, wrapping her arms around his neck to kiss him and hold him tightly. "I'm in love with you. I didn't want to be in love with a rancher, absolutely not the controlling type, which you are. I tried not to be. We're misfits, you and I—two ranchers. I know you think I'm too stubborn and maybe I am. Am I babbling?" she asked. Without pausing for breath or for his answer, she continued. "I've been miserable without you in my life. You're too take-charge. We'll clash and it won't be any more peaceful in the future than it was in the past—"

"Damn, Lindsay," he said, and kissed her, stopping her chatter. She clung to him, kissing him, pouring out the love that she felt along with joy and relief over his declaration.

Suddenly, she leaned away to look at him, framing his face with her hands. "You really, really love me?"

"I really, really love you. Lindsay, will you marry me?" he asked, holding her close against him with one arm wrapped around her waist.

Her heart thudded. "Yes," she gasped. "Oh, yes, Tony. We'll fight, but we'll be in love."

"We might not fight," he whispered. "We may learn to negotiate." She heard the laughter in his voice. He wrapped his fingers in her hair and tugged lightly so she had to look at him. Startled, her eyes flew wide as she looked up at him.

"Will you marry me?" he repeated.

"Yes, I will," she answered.

"Then I'm the happiest man in the world tonight," he said. "I don't care about the differences and I can cope with you and you can cope with me. You'll get used to this rancher, darlin'. You may not get used to my take-charge ways, but we'll work things out because I promise to try to keep you happy. I promise to shower you with love so you won't ever regret marrying an alpha male cowboy."

"Shh, Tony. Stop making wild promises you can't keep," she said, laughing, trailing light kisses over his face. "I love you, cowboy. I love you with all my heart."

He kissed her, a kiss of joy and promise, a kiss that melted her heart and ignited desire again, and soon she was lost in passion.

It was almost ten when she sat with him in her tub while hot water swirled around them and he held her close between his legs as she leaned back against him.

"Hungry? I was going to cook steaks."

"I hadn't thought about it," she said. "I don't know about hunger, but I'm shriveling up from being in this hot water so long."

He chuckled, cupping her full breasts in his hands to caress her. "Not too shriveled," he said. "We'll get out, dry and go eat something. I know you have something in this house and if you don't, we'll head to my place." With big splashes, he stood, pulling her up with him and helping her step out of the tub. He picked up a towel and began slow, light strokes to dry her.

She caught the towel, wrapping it around herself and picking up another folded one to hand to him. "If you keep doing that, we'll end up in bed again. I'll dry myself and you do the same, then get dressed and I'll meet you downstairs. I'm getting hungry and for some reason, I can't skip meals like I used to be able to."

Nodding, he grinned. "Not as much fun, but I'll cooperate."

When he met her downstairs in her kitchen, she already had a casserole heating and in minutes it was on the table. His fingers closed on her wrist and she looked up at him, startled.

"Darlin', I had this evening planned and it hasn't gone the way I expected from the moment you opened the door. But I came prepared for whatever happened." He reached into a pocket, pulled out a small folded bit of tissue paper tied with a tiny strip of blue ribbon. "This is for you, Lindsay."

Surprised, she looked up at him, giving him a searching look, and then she took it to tug free the bow and open the paper carefully, her heart drumming as she did. She looked at a dazzling ring. "Oh, Tony," she gasped, thrilled to look at the ring he had for her. It was a huge, emerald-cut diamond, surrounded by sapphires and diamonds with more diamonds scattered on the gold band.

He took it from her and held her hand. "One more time, the way I should have done it the first time. Lindsay Calhoun, will you marry me?"

"Oh, yes," she replied, laughing. "Yes." She threw her arms around him after he slipped the ring on her finger. Wrapping her arms around his neck, she kissed him and he held her tightly, kissing her in return.

When they finally stopped, he took her hand to walk to the table. "Lindsay, you need to eat. Let's sit and eat and talk about when we'll have a wedding. I hope we can agree on a date soon. Very, very soon."

He held her chair and then sat facing her. She could

barely think about eating because of the excitement and joy churning in her.

"Tony, I've missed you so and I realized I've been in love with you for a long time. I don't know how marriage will work with the two of us, but I can't wait to try."

"You'll be you and I'll still be me. We're in love, so we'll work it out." He grinned and picked up her hand to brush kisses over her knuckles. "I love you, darlin'. Back to the date. Lindsay, let's get married soon. Really soon.

She stared at him and then nodded. "In that, we're in agreement. The sooner the better for so many reasons, not the least of which is I love you with all my heart."

His eyes took on the greenish hue that she recognized from moments of intense emotion or passion. He held her hand and, without taking his gaze from hers, lifted it to his lips to brush more kisses lightly over it.

"Lindsay, I love you and I always will."

"Even if we fight?"

"Even if we fight. But I don't think we really will." He wagged his brows and grinned. "Well, maybe sometimes."

"Now, do you want a surprise?" she asked.

"I think my entire life will be filled with surprises. What's this one, darlin'?"

"It's early, and I'll have an ultrasound later this month, but my doctor thinks I may be having twins."

Stunned, he stared at her. "Twins?" He got up and walked around the table to reach down and draw her to her feet to kiss her hard. When he released her, he grinned. "Lindsay, why do I think my whole life will be like this night? One shock and one change after another."

"You know it won't be that way all the time."

"Get a calendar and let's have this wedding this month."

"Savannah's baby is due this month, but I'd like to

have the wedding soon, too. I've waited as long as I want to wait without you in my life. I don't ever want to go without you again," she said, holding him tightly.

He slipped his hand behind her head and leaned close to kiss her, a long kiss that made her want to be in his arms again and forget wedding plans.

"Tony," she whispered.

"Go get a calendar or I'll get my phone and we'll look at my calendar."

"I have one here." She turned to open a cabinet and came back with a calendar.

With it on the table between them, they discussed dates while they ate.

"After dinner we can call our parents and then start calling our siblings."

"Tony, I love you and I'm so happy."

"I'll show you how I feel in a little while," he said, smiling at her.

Her phone played a tune and she got up to answer it. "Sorry. Anyone calling at this hour has to have a good reason."

"Or a wrong number," he remarked, pulling the calendar close.

She picked up her phone and listened before turning to come back to the table. "That was Mike. Savannah went into labor and they didn't make it to Dallas. She delivered a little girl in the Verity hospital." She couldn't stop the smile that lit up her face. "Wyatt met him at the hospital to get Scotty. He said he texted me earlier, but he didn't hear back. He wants me to come to the hospital to see their baby. Mike sounds incredibly happy."

Tony pulled his chair close beside her. "Sit for a minute and let's pick a date so we can tell everyone and you can show them your ring."

"I don't want to detract from the baby," she said.

He gave her a look. "You're not going to. Babies are wonderful. We're probably not going to surprise anyone. We'll just announce it before we tell everyone goodbye. I didn't intend to walk in and say 'look at us,'" he said.

"You win," she said, smiling at him. "I can't keep it quiet anyway. Well, now we don't have to worry about our wedding interfering with Savannah having her baby."

Tony took her hand. "Lindsay, I want you to have a big wedding, the one you always dreamed of as a little girl. This is once in a lifetime. You won't do it again, I guarantee it."

She gazed at him and then turned to kiss him lightly. "Sometimes you're a very nice man even when you're bossy."

He smiled at her. "Don't sound so surprised." He tapped the calendar. "Pick a date so we can go see your new niece and the happy family."

Eleven

On the first Saturday in November, Lindsay stood in the foyer of the Dallas church watching Scotty walk down the aisle. Dressed in a black tux with black cowboy boots and his hair neatly combed, he was doing just as he had been told. He scattered rose petals along the aisle and took his place at the front by his dad.

Milans and Calhouns were present in abundance. Tony's best man was his older brother Wyatt. Tony had said they would kill the old feud between Calhouns and Milans, so along with his two brothers, he had asked her brothers to be groomsmen and all three accepted. Scotty stood in front of his dad and both of them looked pleased.

Lindsay had asked Savannah if she felt up to being matron of honor. After thanking her, Savannah had declined because of her new baby girl, Caitlin. Lindsay then asked Josh's new wife, Abby, and she accepted instantly, seeming grateful that Lindsay had thought of her. Madi-

son had declined to be a bridesmaid because she was almost into the eighth month of her pregnancy.

"It's time," the wedding planner said, smoothing the
train to Lindsay's white satin dress and checking her veil.
She smiled at Lindsay as her dad took her arm.

"Lindsay, I wish you all the happiness possible," he
said to her as they walked down the long aisle.

"Thanks, Dad," she replied. She looked at Tony in his
black tux and best black boots and her heart beat faster
with joy. She loved him with all her heart. It seemed like
a miracle, something she once thought impossible.

When she joined him at the end of the aisle and met his
gaze, she lost all awareness of their families and friends.
The big Dallas church was filled, but she could see only
Tony.

She repeated her vows, meaning every word, feeling
as if there would be enough love between them to carry
them through any kind of adversity, even the kind they
stirred up themselves.

It seemed a long ceremony, but finally they were pro-
nounced husband and wife. Above a fanfare of trum-
pets, an organ, and applause from the audience, thunder
boomed as they rushed up the aisle.

"Wow," Tony said, glancing over his shoulder at double glass doors. "Is that really thunder?"

"Rain on our wedding day—"

"We had sunshine this morning and rain would be the
best possible thing next to being alone with you within
the hour."

"Rain is more likely to happen than that," she replied,
laughing. "Look how dark it is outside," she said, turning to stare.

"Dare I hope?" Tony replied. "How long will this reception take?"

"Tony, you've asked me that half a dozen times. Hours. It will take hours for me to dance with all the Milan and Calhoun men who are going to ask me to dance because it's the courteous thing to do, much less all the guys who work for me that are here and will be polite and ask me to dance."

"They're not asking because they're polite. This is probably the first time they've seen you look like this and they're having the same kind of reaction I did the night of the auction," he remarked.

"I hope not." A bolt of lightning streaked in a brilliant flash, followed by thunder that rattled windows. Tony grabbed her hand. "C'mere," he said, stepping outside and drawing her beside him as he inhaled deeply.

"Smell that," he said. "And look at the trees. We have an east wind. It's going to rain. Hallelujah!" He yanked her to him to kiss her hard, and for a few minutes she forgot everything else until the first big drop hit her.

"Ki-yi-yippie-ki-ay!" Tony yelled, turning his face up to feel the rain.

"Celebrate inside." She grabbed his hand. "Let's go around where we're supposed to or everyone will be out here and we'll have a mob scene."

They rushed through an empty hall and Tony pulled her into an empty room and closed the door. "Just one more kiss," he said.

"Oh, no. You'll mess us both up for pictures. You have to wait. Come on, Tony," she said, wiggling away and stepping through the door into the hall, smiling and looking away.

"We're coming," she called. "Hurry, Tony."

He stepped out. "Yes, Miss Bossy." He looked down the hall. "Who were you talking to? I don't see a soul.

You made that up to get me out here," he accused, shaking his head but still smiling.

"Come on," she said, laughing and hurrying along the empty hall.

When they passed double glass doors, Tony pulled her to a stop. "Look at that," he said in awe, giving another whoop of joy while she clapped.

"Tony, rain! Finally."

"Just pray it lasts for a week," he said. "What a fantastic wedding gift—rain. Buckets and buckets of rain."

"Reception, remember?" she said, tugging on his hand.

Over an hour later, Tony took her into his arms for their first dance as husband and wife. "Lindsay, you're the most beautiful bride ever. You look even more stunning than the night of the auction," he said, meaning every word. He knew as long as he lived, he would never forget looking at her as she walked down the aisle to marry him.

"Tony, I'm so happy. I didn't think I could ever be this happy."

"Hang on to that as long as you can. I'll try to always make you happy, darlin'."

"Don't make wild promises."

"I'm not. I want you happy. I love you," he said, his arm tightening slightly around her waist as he held her. "Thanks again for agreeing to move into my house. My offer still stands—anytime you want me to build a new house for us, it's fine with me."

She smiled. "I think your house is wonderful," she said. "We'll see, but right now, it looks quite suitable. As long as you love me and you're in my bed at night, what more could I ask for?"

"I wish I could dance you out the door, through that pouring rain, into the limo and off to that bed right now."

"You can't do that. We have to stay and be sociable before we leave for New York."

"I hope you're still happy with going to New York for a few days."

"Very happy. After our babies are born, we can go to Paris and Italy, but I don't want that big a trip right now while I'm pregnant."

"It's your choice, darlin'." He held her close, inhaling the faint scent of her perfume. He just wanted to make her happy because she made him happier than he had ever been in his life.

"Lindsay, we still haven't told anyone we're expecting twins."

"It's just been confirmed and it's still early in my pregnancy. I want to wait a bit. We have time."

"We'll do it however you want," he said, and her blue eyes twinkled.

"I love it when you say that and I hope I hear it millions of times."

He grinned. "I'll try. That's the best I can do, just promise to try. Something I'm trying to resist doing is going out and standing in the rain. I may succumb to that one before we leave."

"Don't you dare. A soggy tux would be dreadful."

"Soggy from rainwater would be dreadful? I beg to differ."

She laughed. "Tony, life is a blast and I intend to enjoy being married to you."

"I'll keep reminding you of that. I'm going to wish I recorded it to play again."

"You still think we're going to fight. I don't think so. You're doing a great job so far of keeping me happy."

He laughed. "You can't imagine how badly I want to get you out of here and all to myself," he said.

"I'll see what I can do about that. Maybe I can hurry things up a bit."

"Darlin', you do know how to please a man."

She felt as if she'd danced with every cowboy in Texas when Mike stepped up to ask her to dance. She smiled at her brother as they danced away.

"Caitlin is a beautiful baby, Mike,"

He grinned. "Thank you. I agree. You look beautiful, too, Lindsay."

"Thank you."

"And happy. I'm glad. Tony's a good guy."

"I agree with you on that one. Savannah said Caitlin is a quiet baby."

"She is and she's a little doll. Someone's holding her constantly. When Mom and Dad arrived, they stayed with us last weekend instead of their usual hotel stay."

"Our mother?"

"Yes, she did. She thinks Caitlin is adorable."

"I'm so glad. She looks like Savannah, even as tiny as she is."

"I agree. I see Jake watching us, so I'm sure he's going to want to dance with you next. I talked to Abe. He's happy for you and he'll run the place just fine while you're gone. I told him if he needs me, call."

"That was nice, thanks," she said. "I've never been away like this."

"It's time you did, Lindsay, and time you got a life of your own. You don't have to get out there and work like one of the boys."

She laughed. "I think those days may be over. Being a mama sounds like a big responsibility."

He smiled at her and danced her toward the sideline. "I'll give you to Jake. You have so many guys who will want to dance with you that you and Tony will never get away."

"Thanks, Mike," she said, planting a kiss on his cheek as they halted and Jake stepped up to take her hand.

Mike was almost right. By the time she'd danced with all the Milans and Calhouns and talked to each of their guests, it was hours later. Finally they made it out of their reception hall.

For just a moment Tony stopped, standing in a downpour and laughing, dancing a jig until she grabbed his wrist and tugged.

They rushed to the waiting limo and fell laughing onto the seat as their chauffeur closed the door.

"The drought will lessen now and your brother told me rain is predicted for the next three days," Tony said, pulling her to him to kiss her before she could answer.

When she pushed him away she laughed as she shook her head. "You're incredibly sexy and appealing, but that wet tux is going to ruin my wedding dress."

"It's rainwater. Do you really care?"

As she shook her head, she laughed until he drew her close to kiss her again.

Tony had a private plane waiting at the airport, but it was the wee hours of the morning when he finally carried her over the threshold into the New York penthouse suite he had reserved for their honeymoon. Standing her on her feet, he pushed away her short charcoal jacket and wrapped his arms around her.

"I love you, Lindsay. I don't think I can ever tell you enough. All I can do is try to show you. I've waited all day for this moment when we would be alone together."

Wrapping her arms around his neck, she smiled at him.

"Mrs. Anthony Milan! It's a whole new life for me. Tony, once again, I am happier than I ever dreamed possible."

His smile vanished as he held her and began to unfasten the buttons down the back of her navy dress. "I hope so and I want to always make you happy, Lindsay. You've filled a huge void in my life. I want to be with you, to love you, to have a family with you. I need you, darlin'."

She tightened her arms around his neck to pull his head down and kiss him. He held her close against him, their hearts beating together.

Joy filled her. She had never known as much contentment as she had found with Tony, and so much excitement as they looked forward to their babies. She couldn't wait to start her new life, a life shared with the man she loved with all her heart—the one rancher in the whole world she could love.

* * * * *

LONE STAR LEGENDS
*Don't miss a single novel
in this Texas-set series from*
USA TODAY *bestselling author Sara Orwig!*

*THE TEXAN'S FORBIDDEN FIANCÉE
A TEXAN IN HER BED
AT THE RANCHER'S REQUEST
KISSED BY A RANCHER
THE RANCHER'S SECRET SON*

All available now, only from Harlequin Desire!

*If you're on Twitter, tell us what you think of
Harlequin Desire! #harlequindesire*

COMING NEXT MONTH FROM

HARLEQUIN Desire

Available February 2, 2016

#2425 His Forever Family
Billionaires and Babies • by Sarah M. Anderson
When caring for an abandoned baby brings Liberty and her billionaire boss Marcus closer, she must resist temptation. Her secrets could destroy her career and the chance to care for the foster child they are both coming to love...

#2426 The Doctor's Baby Dare
Texas Cattleman's Club: Lies and Lullabies
by Michelle Celmer
Dr. Parker Reese always gets what he wants, especially when it comes to women. When a baby shakes up his world, he decides he wants sexy nurse Clare Connelly... Will he have to risk his guarded heart to get her?

#2427 His Pregnant Princess Bride
Bayou Billionaires • by Catherine Mann
What starts as a temporary vacation fling for an arrogant heir to a Southern football fortune and a real-life princess becomes way more than they bargained for when the princess becomes pregnant!

#2428 How to Sleep with the Boss
The Kavanaghs of Silver Glen • by Janice Maynard
Ex-heiress Libby Parkhurst has nothing to lose when she takes a demanding job with Patrick Kavanagh, but her desire to impress the boss is complicated when his matchmaking family gives her a makeover that makes Patrick lose control.

#2429 Tempted by the Texan
The Good, the Bad and the Texan • by Kathie DeNosky
Wealthy rancher Jaron Lambert wants more than just one night with Mariah Stanton, but his dark past and their age difference hold him back. What will it take to push past his boundaries? Mariah's about to find out...

#2430 Needed: One Convenient Husband
The Pearl House • by Fiona Brand
To collect her inheritance, Eva Atraeus only has three weeks to marry. Billionaire banker Kyle Messena, the trustee of the will *and* her first love, rejects every potential groom...until he's the only one left! How convenient...

YOU CAN FIND MORE INFORMATION ON UPCOMING HARLEQUIN® TITLES, FREE EXCERPTS AND MORE AT WWW.HARLEQUIN.COM.

HDCNM0116

REQUEST YOUR FREE BOOKS!
2 FREE NOVELS PLUS 2 FREE GIFTS!

HARLEQUIN®

Desire

ALWAYS POWERFUL, PASSIONATE AND PROVOCATIVE

YES! Please send me 2 FREE Harlequin® Desire novels and my 2 FREE gifts (gifts are worth about $10). After receiving them, if I don't wish to receive any more books, I can return the shipping statement marked "cancel." If I don't cancel, I will receive 6 brand-new novels every month and be billed just $4.55 per book in the U.S. or $5.24 per book in Canada. That's a savings of at least 13% off the cover price! It's quite a bargain! Shipping and handling is just 50¢ per book in the U.S. and 75¢ per book in Canada.* I understand that accepting the 2 free books and gifts places me under no obligation to buy anything. I can always return a shipment and cancel at any time. Even if I never buy another book, the two free books and gifts are mine to keep forever.

225/326 HDN GH2P

Name _____ (PLEASE PRINT)

Address _____ Apt. #

City _____ State/Prov. _____ Zip/Postal Code

Signature (if under 18, a parent or guardian must sign)

Mail to the **Reader Service:**
IN U.S.A.: P.O. Box 1867, Buffalo, NY 14240-1867
IN CANADA: P.O. Box 609, Fort Erie, Ontario L2A 5X3

Want to try two free books from another line?
Call 1-800-873-8635 or visit www.ReaderService.com.

* Terms and prices subject to change without notice. Prices do not include applicable taxes. Sales tax applicable in N.Y. Canadian residents will be charged applicable taxes. Offer not valid in Quebec. This offer is limited to one order per household. Not valid for current subscribers to Harlequin Desire books. All orders subject to credit approval. Credit or debit balances in a customer's account(s) may be offset by any other outstanding balance owed by or to the customer. Please allow 4 to 6 weeks for delivery. Offer available while quantities last.

Your Privacy—The Reader Service is committed to protecting your privacy. Our Privacy Policy is available online at www.ReaderService.com or upon request from the Reader Service.

We make a portion of our mailing list available to reputable third parties that offer products we believe may interest you. If you prefer that we not exchange your name with third parties, or if you wish to clarify or modify your communication preferences, please visit us at www.ReaderService.com/consumerschoice or write to us at Reader Service Preference Service, P.O. Box 9062, Buffalo, NY 14240-9062. Include your complete name and address.

HD15

SPECIAL EXCERPT FROM

◆ HARLEQUIN®
™

Desire

*While caring for an abandoned baby brings Liberty
and her billionaire boss Marcus closer, her secrets
could destroy her career and the chance to care for the
foster child they are both coming to love…*

Read on for a sneak peek of
HIS FOREVER FAMILY
by **Sarah M. Anderson**

"You have to make a decision about attending the
Hanson wedding."

Marcus groaned. He did not want to watch his former
fiancée get married to the man she'd cheated on him
with. Unfortunately, to some, his inability to see the
truth about Lillibeth until it was too late also indicated an
inability to make good investment choices. So his parents
had strongly suggested he attend the wedding, with an
appropriate date on his arm.

All Marcus had to do was pick a woman.

"The options are limited and time is running short,
Mr. Warren," Liberty said. She jammed her hands on her
hips. "The wedding is in two weeks."

"Fine. I'll take you."

The effect of this statement was immediate. Liberty's
eyes went wide and her mouth dropped open and her gaze
dropped over his body. Something that looked a hell of a
lot like desire flashed over her face.

Then it was gone. She straightened and did her best to
look imperial. "Mr. Warren, be serious."

"I am serious. I trust you." He took a step toward her. "Sometimes I think…you're the only person who's honest with me. I want to take you to the wedding."

It was hard to say if she blushed, as she was already red-faced from their morning run and the heat. But something in her expression changed. "No," she said flatly. Before he could take the rejection personally, she added, "I—it—would be bad for you."

He could hear the pain in her voice. He took another step toward her and put a hand on her shoulder. She looked up, her eyes wide and—hopeful? His hand drifted from her shoulder to her cheek and damned if she didn't lean into his touch. "How could you be bad for me?"

The moment the words left his mouth, he realized he'd pushed this too far.

She shut down. She stepped away and turned to face the lake. "We need to head back to the office."

That's when he heard a noise. Marcus looked around, trying to find the source. A shoe box on the ground next to a trash can moved.

Marcus's stomach fell in. Oh, no—who would throw away a kitten? He hurried over to the box and pulled the lid off and—

Sweet Jesus. Not a kitten.

A baby.

Don't miss
HIS FOREVER FAMILY by Sarah M. Anderson
available February 2016 wherever
Harlequin® Desire books and ebooks are sold.

www.Harlequin.com

Copyright © 2016 by Sarah M. Anderson

HDEXP0116

Turn your love of reading into rewards you'll love with
Harlequin My Rewards

**Join for FREE today at
www.HarlequinMyRewards.com**

Earn **FREE BOOKS** of your choice.

Experience **EXCLUSIVE OFFERS** and contests.

Enjoy **BOOK RECOMMENDATIONS**
selected just for you.

PLUS! Sign up now
and get **500** points
right away!

Earn **FREE** REWARDS
HarlequinMyRewards.com
Join Today!

MYR16R

Love the Harlequin book you just read?

Your opinion matters.

Review this book on your favorite book site, review site, blog or your own social media properties and share your opinion with other readers!

Be sure to connect with us at:
Harlequin.com/Newsletters
Facebook.com/HarlequinBooks
Twitter.com/HarlequinBooks

HREVIEWS

JUST CAN'T GET ENOUGH?

Join our social communities
and talk to us online.

You will have access to the latest
news on upcoming titles and special
promotions, but most importantly,
you can talk to other fans about your
favorite Harlequin reads.

Harlequin.com/Community

f Facebook.com/HarlequinBooks

Twitter.com/HarlequinBooks

P Pinterest.com/HarlequinBooks

HSOCIAL

THE WORLD IS BETTER WITH

Romance

Harlequin has everything from contemporary, passionate and heartwarming to suspenseful and inspirational stories.

Whatever your mood, we have a romance just for you!

Connect with us to find your next great read, special offers and more.

f /HarlequinBooks

🐦 @HarlequinBooks

www.HarlequinBlog.com

www.Harlequin.com/Newsletters

(H) HARLEQUIN®

A *Romance* FOR EVERY MOOD™

www.Harlequin.com

SERIESHALOAD2015